The War, Love, & Harmony Series: Book 3
The Sheik's Secret Bride

Elizabeth Lennox

Note: Books 1 and 2 in The War, Love, & Harmony Series are free e-books. Learn more about the series or download the free books at ElizabethLennox.com.

CONTENTS

About the War, Love, and Harmony Series

This series encompasses two generations of love stories across the four fictional neighboring countries of Larcatia, Altair, Lurasa, and Tularia. When the four betrothed princes and princesses fall in love with the wrong partner, a devastating chain of events is set into motion. Only the future leaders can put things right.

The first two stories tell the tales of two princes and their unplanned romances. These books are available free as e-books from ElizabethLennox.com.

Fighting with the Infuriating Prince: Jalayla couldn't believe the arrogance of the man! To actually order her around? How rude! But beneath the surface of her anger towards the handsome prince, there was a simmering heat, an uninvited fascination with the man that she couldn't seem to fight. Every time he touched her, every time he even looked at her, she felt that strange sensation.

Tasir wanted to fire her at first sight. She argued with him about everything and challenged him in ways that no other woman dared. So why did he want to pick the woman up and make love to her? Initially, he didn't know that the lovely woman with fiery eyes and a sensuous figure was the one and only Princess Jalayla. And was determined that he would have her for his own.

So what's a man to do when he finds out that the woman of his dreams is promised to marry another man?

Dancing with the Dangerous Prince: Jalayla couldn't believe the arrogance of the man! To actually order her around? How rude! But beneath the surface of her anger towards the handsome prince, there was a simmering heat, an uninvited fascination with the man that she couldn't seem to fight. Every time he touched her, every time he even looked at her, she felt that strange sensation.

Tasir wanted to fire her at first sight. She argued with him about everything and challenged him in ways that no other woman dared. So why did he want to pick the woman up and make love to her? Initially, he didn't know that the lovely woman with fiery eyes and a sensuous figure was the one and only Princess Jalayla. And was determined that he would have her for his own.

So what's a man to do when he finds out that the woman of his dreams is promised to marry another man?

Two weddings! Two love matches that weren't supposed to be! Princess Ciara of Altair, previously engaged to Prince Tasir went on to marry Prince Zoran of Larcatia. While Prince Tasir of Lurasa weds Princess Jalayla of Tularia.

Unfortunately, the weddings don't result in peace. The two couples were able to experience only a short-lived interlude of calm before tensions escalated to the point that violence was inevitable. Even after the weddings and despite years of trying to calm the problems, the four countries break out into war. A ten year, brutal war that was never supposed to be.

Sheik Zahir del Hassar Alzar of Larcatia brings the three other ruling sheiks to the Fortress of the Guards in secret. These four men – some recently risen to their power, others who have been rulers for a few years – all agree that it is time to stop the war caused by the tensions that were started when their parents or ancestors married years ago. The fighting has been going on too long and nothing has been gained. Borders remain as they were before the wars took place and the reasons for fighting don't seem to apply any longer. The broken marriage contracts never should have resulted in war; peace must be restored for the benefit of all four countries.

After long and challenging negotiations, the four rulers agree to cease hostilities and sign treaties so that the healing process can begin. They devise a strategy to help their people diffuse the rivalries and tensions that have developed. The four men agree that the best way to show their subjects that life should move on, without war, is to each marry and produce an heir. Royal weddings and the birth of a new generation will give the people a reason to hope.

The saga continues with another generation, where the now-current rulers of Larcatia, Altair, Lurasa, and Tularia must fulfill their treaty obligations.

The Sheik's Secret Bride: Their story began five years ago. Callie fell madly, crazily in love with Zahir. But the war in his country was raging and nurturing their relationship was tenuous at best. When Callie was captured, the experience was terrifying. Zahir found and rescued her, but he knew it would be impossible to insulate her from danger in his country. Despite his wishes to be together, he knew that to keep her safe he must send her away. However, he wouldn't let her go until she was his bride. In a secret wedding, he married her, and then spirited her to safety.

She arrived in her haven traumatized, fearful, homeless...and pregnant. Slowly, she rebuilt her life, gave birth to her son and somehow learned to get on with living without Zahir. For five long years, Callie recovered from the nightmare of her captivity. And she raises her son.

When Zahir enters her life once more, she can't believe that the fire between them is hotter than before. But she refuses to give in, despite its intensity. She's too afraid that the peace between the previously warring countries will end and that she or her son could be in peril again. She yearns to feel safe, but can she defy her heart or deny her son his father?

The Sheik's Angry Bride: Duty. Responsibility. Those were the priorities of Layla's upbringing. So when her father announced that she is to marry the Sheik of Lurasa, she accepted her duty and steeled her heart to a loveless life of obligation.

What she refused to accept was Garon's intense effect on her. The man wasn't what she anticipated! And he wouldn't conform to her plans or expectations. This was an arranged marriage! They had appearances to maintain, duties to adhere to. Why were these crazy feelings flying between them every time he touched her?

Garon entered into the marriage expecting only to be faithful to his wife and to the agreement he had made with the other sheiks. What he wasn't expecting was a fiery beauty that set his senses on fire or the intense need to have her. Responsibility be damned, this woman was his! And he was going to teach her about living and loving.

The Sheik's Blackmailed Bride: Luna couldn't believe the chain of events that had led to her wedding day. All she'd wanted was to save her small village, to help the residents to get out from underneath their crippling debt. So she'd written to the man who owned the bank. And here she was, walking down the aisle toward a man she barely knew. A man who could make her body sing but who could crush her hopes and dreams with a few harsh words.

Dassar needed a wife. The lovely Luna fit none of his criteria. She was too soft, too sweet and would be hurt by palace life. So why couldn't he forget her? Why could she get under his skin so easily? And why couldn't he simply walk away?

The Sheik's Convenient Bride: The only reason Kylie had come back to the palace was to prove to everyone that she was over Tarek. Her girlish infatuation was a thing of the past. So how did she end up dining with the sheik? And why was her body still vibrating when he kissed her? Why couldn't she simply put her infatuation in the past where it belonged?

Tarek took one look at the fascinating beauty and knew that Kylie was the woman he was going to have for his wife. He didn't want to marry, but the terms of the peace treaty were absolute. So if he had to do it, why not do it with the lovely, feisty and sexy woman that he couldn't get out of his mind?

Note to readers: Although the books of the series are related by this shared backstory, each is an independent story in its own right. With the preceding context for reference, the books may be read out of order. Books 1 and 2 are free e-books and may be downloaded from ElizabethLennox.com.

Prologue

Sheik Zahir del Hassar Alzar watched with almost savage anticipation as the last of the documents were signed. When the pen was finally dropped onto the desk, there was an almost tangible sigh of relief. Four rulers, all their aides and staff members as well as the personal guards standing sentry, understood the significance of that last signature.

There was a moment when every person stood silent, each person within that room looking around as the implication was absorbed.

Zahir nodded to his body guard who understood the signal. "It is done," he said quietly but with a satisfaction that was so intense, he felt like pounding something. Instead, he stood still, looking at the other three men at the table. They were all leaders of their respective countries now, all just as tall as he was and none were afraid to fight for their people. But Zahir could also sense that they understood that this war had to end.

"It is agreed. Marriage and heirs," Zahir said despite the fact that everyone had just signed their name, agreeing to the terms.

The other three men nodded.

Zahir turned and lifted one of the four celebratory glasses of thirty-year-old Isle of Jura scotch, waiting for the other three men to do the same. Their battle-scarred hands lifted their glasses into the air. "To peace," he said. Simple and yet profound.

"To peace," the other three agreed, just as somberly before clinking glasses.

Zahir looked at each of the men as they sipped their drinks. He'd grown to respect each of these men over the past few months. They'd all agreed to negotiate the peace treaty, just the four of them. It had been an unprecedented act for each be at the negotiation table himself instead of sending representatives. But the secret fort, built on the point where all four of their countries met, had been the perfect place to end this violent, ten year war. It had also been the place where the animosity had started with the dissolution of marriage contracts had started much of the animosity so their efforts, culminating in the treaty today, were significant.

"I've arranged a celebratory dinner for tonight," Zahir said.

Sheik Tarek bin Faisal of Tularia nodded his head. "We are celebrating marriage?" he teased.

Two of the other men laughed, agreeing with him but Zahir only smiled. "Ah, gentlemen. I hope that each of you find a woman like my Callie," he told them all, startling the three men who were dreading the loss of their freedom but accepting that it was their duty and responsibility. Not just for the treaty but for their countries as well. They were all in their thirties, past time for them to marry and produce an heir so the line of succession would not be in question.

"I just hope to get the task over with quickly," Sheik Garon Al Sharhi of Lurasa stated with grim acceptance.

"To a wife and an heir," Sheik Dassar bin Sarook of Altair replied with equal cheerless acquiescence. "May they all be beautiful and gracious."

Tarek chuckled. "When word of this gets out, all the pretty little gold-diggers of the world are going to be on our doorsteps," he forecasted with revulsion. "How about if we all agree to keep our matrimonial plans private until we've selected our appropriate bride?" He turned to Zahir. "Three of us aren't as lucky to have married years ago. You're fortunate you don't have to start the search now."

Zahir's lips compressed. "We all have our challenges," he told the three of them. No other words needed to be spoken. These men knew what had happened to his wife five years ago. None had approved either, which was one of the reasons why Zahir respected these men so intensely. They all believed in keeping hostilities between combatants. They had all fought hard, but with honor. And all of them had approached the peace negotiations with determination, none believing that the war was good for any of their countries.

"To peace," Zahir said again and all four men downed the thirty year old scotch with appreciation.

As the celebration dinner commenced with enormous amounts of food, excellent wine and dancers for entertainment, Zahir sat back and watched with a fierce sense of pride that the peace treaty was signed as well as an almost savage impatience to get to his woman, to bring her back to his home.

And to meet his son!

Chapter 1

"Hello Callie."

Callie heard the deep voice but her arms, still loaded down with the items of daily life, didn't move. Not a muscle in her body moved.

At first her heart soared, excitement ripped through her mind and body. He was here! He came back for her! She almost turned to throw herself into his strong arms, but then the painful memories, the horror and fear of those terrible days in his country....

There was a pause, a pregnant moment when nothing in the world moved. Possibly even the earth stopped rotating because her excitement swiftly changed to paralyzing fear.

That voice. It was impossible! He couldn't be here, she told herself even as her arms started shaking from the effort of holding everything. It simply wasn't possible that he was here. Not this man, not now. Things had been going so well! This man would...well, things would change!

The mail, her purse, computer bag and groceries that had been precariously balanced in her arms suddenly tumbled to the floor as the world mercilessly started moving again. "No!" she whispered with both anguish and that silly, irrational hope that she'd tried very hard to obliterate over the past five years.

As she slowly straightened up, she whispered, "Please, please, please, please," as if her begging could diminish the possibility of the one man with that incredible voice standing in her apartment at this moment.

Life had been going so beautifully lately, she simply would not allow for the possibility that he was standing here. The last time he'd come into her life, her world had gone out of control. She'd fallen madly in love with that man and followed him from the United States to his beautiful country. For a few weeks, they'd been deliriously happy and she couldn't believe her luck in finding a man as tall, strong and handsome, wondering what he could possibly see in her. But on a normal trip through the exciting Saturday market where she'd started to learn about his country and the people, she'd been kidnapped, tossed into a dark hole for three days and, at the end of it all, she'd come back to the relative safety of the United

States. As if being kidnapped and traumatized, then ripped from the arms of the man she loved more than life itself wasn't bad enough, she'd discovered that she was also alone, homeless and...pregnant.

She'd turned her life around. She now had a job she loved, a warm, comfortable place to come home to every night and friends, not to mention her adorable little boy who gave her so much happiness. Life was good. And no matter how amazing the sex had been with this man, no matter how shockingly wonderful he had made her feel or how alive and vibrant her life had become for those short weeks she'd been in his company, she would never go back to that world. She could never let this man back into her life. She wouldn't do that to her son or to herself.

When she was once again able to breathe, she looked up, almost afraid – maybe afraid that he was here or perhaps that he wasn't. Her mind might be adamant that this man was not coming back into her life, but her body was remembering what it was like to be touched by this man. To be held in his arms. Good grief, just listening to him had been a turn on because of his deep voice that felt like naughty thoughts sliding over her skin whenever he spoke. He could be droning on about oil prices or treaties and her whole body would start tingling. It had been embarrassing the last time they'd been together because he could so easily break down her resistance.

Resistance. That was a laugh, she thought as she slowly turned to find the man through the dim light of the fading afternoon sunlight, praying that it wasn't really him. Because she had zero resistance where this man was concerned. He had powers over her that could make her knees tremble from just a look.

"You're not here," she said to the image standing in her living room. "You can't be here."

Zahir watched the woman that had haunted his dreams as she slowly straightened. She'd lost weight, he noticed. But she was still as beautiful as he remembered. And she still had the most powerful effect on his body just by her presence. He'd never been able to control his body's response to this woman. She was like a drug that had become an addiction to him. A drug he'd had to send away to protect.

But it was safe now. And he was determined to claim his woman.

Her words were soft and her full, pink lips rounded in surprise as she confronted him. Even as he stood there, he couldn't believe how quickly his body hardened just at the sight of her. She was truly beautiful with her thick blond hair and her almost golden eyes. They were actually brown, he remembered, but the golden flecks changed the color, making them appear lighter during certain moods. Her eyes had always fascinated him and he wanted to pull her into his arms right now, make love to her and bring her back to his country so that he could rediscover all those secret places that had fascinated him five years ago.

He restrained himself from his initial instinct, his need to toss her over his shoulder and carry her out of this place. He had to be careful with her. She'd been traumatized the last time he'd brought her to his home. He would have to show her that she could trust him, prove that she would be safe. As much as he wanted her, in his home and in his bed, proving that she was safe would take time.

"I'm here, Callie," he replied softly, urgently.

She shook her head, a few glossy, golden wisps of hair caressing her neck and shoulders. "No. You're not here."

Zahir moved closer and she stepped back, forgetting the mess surrounding her feet. When she stumbled on her purse, he was quick to reach out and catch her but she pushed his hands away, shaking her head and causing those gorgeous tresses to tumble out of the clip that had been holding them on top of her head. The sunny locks fell down her neck and floated around her shoulders like a golden, silken cloud.

"Don't touch me," she gasped as she found her footing once again. "Just get out of my apartment," she ordered him. She leaned up against the wall, not sure if her legs would hold her upright much longer.

"The war is over," he told her, needing her to know. There was so much he had to tell her, but the most important issue was that the war was over and she would be safe. Safe with him.

Callie stopped cold, her amber eyes sweeping up to his with hope and yearning. "Over?" she whispered. She couldn't believe it. The war had been going on for ten, long, ghastly years! How could it just be over? The trembling that she'd felt initially rushed back with volcanic force, making her fingers shake so badly she had to hide them behind her back, not wanting him to see how intensely that news, as well as his presence, affected her.

He moved a step closer and Callie was stunned anew at how tall he was. And how muscular! And handsome! Goodness, he was so tall and both his height as well as all of those packed muscles on his body never failed to make her feel small and feminine. She'd fought that sensation when they'd first met, thinking she needed to be strong in order to be a woman. But she'd quickly discovered that it was pointless when he was close. Every part of her knew that she was soft and feminine when he was close. Every part of her trembled in anticipation of how he would make all of her femininity scream out with joy and excitement when he was close.

Zahir nodded his dark head, his chestnut brown eyes searching hers and she could see those eyes even in the shadows cast by the descending sun. "Over." He affirmed firmly. "There has been a dramatic change in the leadership of the other three countries over the past few years which allowed the negotiations to begin. A peace treaty was signed by all four countries last week. It is over."

That news was like a song bursting for joy in her heart but she mercilessly tamped down that delight. She couldn't believe in the peace, she told herself firmly. She'd naively followed him to his home the last time, thinking that everything would be roses and sunshine and that innocent dream had been shattered when that disgusting thug had simply lifted her up as she'd examined the spices in the marketplace, dumping her into the trunk of a car and driving off with her. The guards that had been assigned to protect her hadn't been able to do a thing to stop the abductors and Callie had been too weak to do anything. Too weak and too scared! But never again! She was stronger now. She was not going to be weak ever again!

Pushing those paralyzing thoughts out of her mind, she confronted him, not even trying to hide the emotions in her body or her tone. "How long?" she asked, her body trembling at the idea of being in his arms again, of being free to love this man. If the war was over then.... "No! It doesn't matter," she said firmly, squinching up her eyes in an effort to get her mind back on the right track. "Wars have stopped and started again. Besides, it is over between us."

Zahir moved closer, his eyes darkening even more as he recognized both her fears and her desires. "The war is over, Callie. And we're going to be together again."

She shook her head, unaware of how that caused her hair to shimmer in the overhead light. "It's never over. You have been at war with your enemies for far too long. Your people don't know how to live with peace. They'll come up with some reason to start fighting again. And I won't go back. I don't want you and I will not endure that life ever again."

He moved closer, hearing her gasp as he put a hand on either side of her head against the wall behind her. He wasn't holding back now. Every fiber of his enormous body emanated the innate authority that had been such a powerful aphrodisiac five years ago. But she fought that feeling, fought against the melting desire to throw herself into his arms and feel his strong muscles hold her gently against his massive chest.

Zahir watched those beguiling amber eyes, seeing everything in them as well as in the subtle movement of her lips and her speeding heart rate on her neck just underneath that soft, tender skin. He would not let her back away from him though. This was his woman and she had to understand that they were meant to be together. He'd worked hard to get them to this place and he wasn't going to let her ignore the way she felt for him just because she was scared.

"The war is over. The last of the old guard died six months ago. I've spent every moment since then working with the rulers of the other three countries, building up a peace agreement. That agreement is signed, sealed and delivered. In addition, the people of our countries are sick of wars, sick of their sons and daughters dying. They want peace. They all want to build their towns up again, to live without fear, to walk down the street or go to the market and not be afraid of being attacked. And I'm going to make that happen."

"How?" she demanded. "You saying it won't make it so!" she panicked because he was so close and he smelled so good! Her fingers ached to reach out and touch him, to feel his warm skin and run her fingers across the stubble already forming on his hard jawline. This man, and only this man, could make her feel like this. And she had to fight it. She couldn't go through that again.

Besides, she had Luca to worry about now. She refused to let him be raised in a country where violence was always the answer. He was four years old and the most amazing little man. She was a mother now and she had to protect her child.

She just had to fight against his appeal. She reminded herself that she was stronger now. She'd learned the hard way what could happen when she ignored caution. She could ignore this! She had to! His confidence might make her shiver - as did that voice - but she tamped down those feelings. In the past, those two aspects of this man had been a powerful aphrodisiac, never failing to make her body respond but right now, she needed to just push him out of her life.

Zahir perceived the battle she was waging inside of her and realized that this would be harder than he'd anticipated. His beautiful Callie wasn't the naïve, sweet, trusting woman she'd been five years ago. Oh, she was still shockingly beautiful, so much so that it made him ache to keep his hands off of her. But he had to gain her trust first. That was the most important thing right now.

"The peace will hold. I have secret meetings every three months with the rulers of the other countries involved, more often if something happens to threaten the peace even slightly. It is done. The other three rulers are just as determined to push this behind them as I am. We are all working very hard to rebuild our economies, our cities and villages. We will make this work," he told her forcefully.

She shook her head, both to stop his words as well as to stop the thrilling impact of his nearness. "I don't believe you."

"It is over." His hand moved to her hair, his fingers tangling in her blond tresses. "It's over," he repeated adamantly. "We can get on with our lives."

A moment later, his mouth covered hers. She tried to resist. She truly did. She stood there, trying to not react, to ignore the heart-pounding, desperate need that surfaced with his touch and bubbled throughout her whole body. But this was Zahir. She'd never been able to resist him. Never. And this time was no different.

The kiss went on and on and her whole body pressed against his, needing more than just his lips against her mouth. For five years she'd suppressed her need, ignored her dreams and refused to let herself even think about how he could make her feel. So this kiss, his hands on her waist and her back, made five years of brutally suppressed yearning spring to life inside of her, almost choking her with the need that this man could so effortlessly generate within her.

With a sob, her head tilted forward, resting on his chest. "Don't do this," she begged. "Please, just walk away and pretend that you never saw...me." She almost slipped and told him about Luca but she knew that if he found out about his son, he would never leave here. Five years ago, when she'd been so rapturously happy just being with him, they'd actually talked about children, about how another generation might give his people hope and pull them out of the war.

In response to her pleas, he lifted her head and his mouth covered hers once more. She couldn't stop him and after a moment, she didn't want to. It had been so long, so very long, since a man had touched her. She whimpered, her hands reaching up and clutching the silk of his dress shirt as if it were a life line. She held him there, kissing him and waiting for him to lift her into his arms and carry her to the bedroom, to make love to her as he had so often in the past.

The ringing interrupted them, although she had no idea how long the phone had been going off but he lifted his head, his arm wrapping around her and holding her close even while she snuggled up against his chest. She was shivering and trying to think creatively about how to handle this situation. She simply couldn't be swept away by this man again. She had to protect their son!

While he spoke to the person on the other end of the phone, she stood there in the circle of his arms, enjoying, for the last time, the strength of him wrapped around her. This had been her man. She'd built dreams around him, wanting to marry him from the first moment she'd seen him, the first time he'd spoken to her. And for weeks, she'd thought he felt the same way. She'd gone with him, flown out of the country to be with him only to discover that his life was too hard for her. She had been too weak.

Zahir muttered a curse as he ended the call and slipped the phone back into his pocket. Callie was still in his arms and she was softer than he remembered, more amazingly feminine and all he wanted to do was ignore that phone call and lose himself in her arms once more. But the call was urgent and he couldn't ignore his responsibilities. "I have to go, but I'll be back." He bent and kissed her forehead.

She heard the words and felt cold, almost desolate, with his strong arms no longer around her. But the absence of his touch gave her back rational thinking and she shook her head, remembering all the reasons why she had to be strong and resist him now. "This has to end, Zahir," she told him and pulled out of his arms, grateful when he allowed it. She knew he was strong enough to hold her but she moved several feet away, wrapping her arms around herself. "You have to go away and leave me alone."

He answered by swiftly shaking his head and pulling her back into his arms, her soft, full breasts pressing against his hard chest and his dark eyes boring into hers.

"This isn't over and there's no way I'm leaving you. I'll just have to show you that this can work, that the peace will hold. And eventually, you will trust me, Callie."

A moment later, he was gone and she shivered at the stillness of the room. When Zahir was around, the air practically vibrated with his energy. He was like a live wire and she'd become addicted to his power, to his energy.

Goodness, it had taken so long for her to recover from that man the first time.

"Momma!" Luca's voice called out.

Callie turned around and bent lower just in time for her son to throw himself into her arms. She grabbed him and held him tight, eager to see him and hold him. "Hi there, buddy!" she said, running her fingers through his hair. Not for the first time did she notice how similar Luca's hair was to Zahir's. And his eyes as well as several of those endearing mannerisms that only alpha males, or soon-to-be alpha males, could get away with.

Always sensitive to her emotions, Luca's pudgy hands moved to each side of her face so he could look directly into her eyes. "What's wrong, Momma?" he asked, pulling away slightly so his dark eyes could see her more clearly. She almost started crying when his lips compressed in that manner, just like his father's had done only moments ago. "Are you okay?" he asked, his dark eyebrows furrowing with worry.

"I'm fine," she said, laughing at how cute he looked. "What did you do today?' she asked.

"I read Harry Potter!" he exclaimed, eager to tell her about his day. "Did you know that he's magic?"

Callie laughed, delighted with his enthusiasm but more than a little stunned that he was reading something as complicated as the wizard story. She put him down and picked up all of the mail that had scattered across the floor. Storing her computer against the wall and her keys on the hook, she dumped the mail on the counter, nodding her head as she listened to Luca describe all of the problems the famous wizard had gotten into on his first day at magic school. Unfortunately, she couldn't focus all of her attention on his excited chatter. Her mind was too amazed, stunned, horrified and....okay, she admitted that she was excited to see Zahir, but she ignored that defiant emotion trying to get through to her consciousness and focused on how she was going to avoid Zahir the next time he came around. Perhaps she could take a vacation. Just go away for the weekend? Maybe he would get the idea that she really was serious about them not getting back together.

She was busy making dinner when she suddenly realized that there was silence behind her. She glanced around and saw Luca sitting on a stool staring at her. "What's wrong?" she asked, her hand holding the spoon carefully over the pot of boiling water.

Luca's brown eyes crinkled up with laughter. "Momma, why did you just pour cereal into the pot?"

Callie stared at her son for a moment, trying to understand what he was saying. "What do you mean?" she finally asked.

He nodded his head towards the boiling water and Callie spun back around to the stove. Sure enough, instead of bow tie pasta in the water, there were a bunch of whole-wheat circles bobbing up and down.

"And I don't think tuna fish in the spaghetti sauce is a good idea, Momma."

Callie's eyes dropped to the saucepan right next to the pot of now-mushy cereal. Yep, tuna fish and spaghetti sauce. "Disgusting," she sighed and her shoulders sagged. Turning to face her little man, she forced a smile on her face and said, "Let's go out to eat!"

Luca's face split into a huge grin and he threw up his hands. "Yes!" and he jumped off of the stool. Callie cringed, thinking he was just too little to do that but he was such a sturdy little guy.

She grabbed her purse and keys and they stomped out of the building. At their favorite restaurant, Callie ordered a salad without dressing and Luca ordered a burger with fries, his favorite since she rarely cooked burgers herself.

"Why are you eating a salad, Momma?" he asked as he took a bite of his burger.

"Oh, you know, just trying to be healthy."

He looked at her with a knowing glance. "You're trying to lose weight again, aren't you?"

Her lips pulled back into a cringe. "What do you know about trying to lose weight?" she asked. She'd tried to hide all of her little secrets from him, including her fear of gaining weight. She'd been pretty good about it up until an hour ago. But with Zahir back in the picture, she was suddenly conscious of her weight, wondering if she'd put on pounds lately since she hadn't had time to get to the gym.

He only shook his head again and laid a sacred fry on the edge of her salad bowl. "You're beautiful, Momma," he told her. "Ms. Fisher told me I have to say that anytime I see a woman dieting." He nodded his head for emphasis…and then took an enormous bite of his burger. Callie had to laugh. There were startling moments of brilliance from this little guy, then he reverted back to his precious, four-year-old mind-set.

Goodness, she loved this boy, she thought. Which only reinforced her desire to protect him by staying away from Zahir.

Chapter 2

"So? Are you going to accept?"

Callie looked up from her computer, taking a long moment to focus on the woman standing in her doorway. Ever since Zahir had come back last night, it had been a constant struggle to focus. So when her friend walked in and sat down in the chair in front of her desk, Callie wasn't sure what they were talking about. "Accept?" she asked. Her mind had been far away, memories of both last night as well as five years ago swamping her mind, not allowing her to focus on today's priorities.

Laura laughed and took a seat in the chair in front of Callie's desk. "Yeah. Are you going to accept if he asks you out finally?"

"Who are we talking about?" she asked, narrowing her eyes as she tried to think back to previous conversations, but her mind was a blank other than the worry that Zahir could walk into this office at any moment. Was it possible that he knew where she worked?

Her mind instantly scoffed at that question. The man was ruler of his country with a security staff that protected him non-stop. Of course he knew where she worked!

"The delivery guy!" Laura came right back with an excited wiggle in her chair. "The one with the buff arms and the smile whenever you sign for a package? That one?"

Callie sighed as she glanced down at a file on her desk, trying to remember what was going on and who Laura was talking about. Was there really a delivery guy that smiled at her? And would that smile be better than Zahir's? Callie rubbed her forehead, trying to figure out what to say and do. Everything felt like a struggle from moment to moment today.

A voice from her doorway stopped her before she could form reply. "Laura, how is the design going for the Trundle account?" their boss asked, referring to the web design that Callie had assigned to Laura. "Isn't it due tomorrow?"

Laura grimaced but only Callie saw the disrespectful expression. "It's almost finished," the younger woman said, standing up and walking out of the office quickly, ducking around the lioness that managed the company. Marcia was an amazing boss, always available for help and words of wisdom, and she was fiercely protective of all of her employees. But she was also a stickler for protocol, emphatic about work ethic and pushed all of her employees to strive for a higher level of excellence. It showed in their output and in the way the company had grown over the years, but Laura still wished that the dragon lady would relax every once in a while.

Marcia watched Laura hurry down the hallway for a moment before turning to face Callie again. "Do you have a new boyfriend?" she teased, completely changing the subject.

The image of Zahir popped into her mind but she quickly banished that possibility. Zahir could never be a part of her future. She'd been too hurt in the past and she couldn't venture into that country again. Never!

Instead, Callie snorted as she shook her head. "In order to have a 'new' boyfriend, I'd have to have had an 'old' boyfriend. And since it feels like my entire world is made up of women and very," she paused as Tom walked by her office doorway, "strange men," referring to Tom's odd habits which included taxidermy and entomology, "it isn't very easy to find a date."

Callie leaned back in her chair with a resigned sigh. Thinking that finding a man who could replace Zahir might be a good idea, she tapped a pen against her nose, trying to come up with a plan of action. "Maybe I should just use the online dating services. It would definitely broaden my pool of available men." Callie didn't see Marcia's body stiffen with her words but she'd heard her friend's and boss' concerns about the online dating world before. "I know that you have several friends who have gotten hurt by the men they found online, but really, I'm getting a bit desperate." Especially now that Zahir was back. She had to find a way to resist him! She just had to! Perhaps a new man would banish, or at least diminish, Zahir's impact on her.

Marcia smiled gently and sat down in the chair Laura had just vacated. "I wish I knew of some available men. I'd set you up with one of them in a heartbeat." She paused. "I think what you really need is a change of scenery. You need a vacation." She held up her hand even as Callie opened her mouth to protest. "I'm now making this an order, Callie. You haven't had a vacation in two years. And that adorable little boy of yours deserves an interesting expedition. You've been saving up for a trip to Disney World for years. Why not just head down to Florida? And if you don't want to go there, then you are going to my parents' lake house. It's just two hours away and gorgeous. You'll be close enough to Luca's doctors if something happens, which it won't, and you'll be able to swim and relax and enjoy the sunsets with a huge margarita in your hands. I'll even give the housekeeper free rein to cook up anything she likes so you won't need to cook. How's that?"

Callie was almost salivating at the thought of, not just a vacation, but a way to get away from Zahir. Marcia was right about the relaxing though. It had been a long time. In fact, her last vacation had been two years ago and she'd only taken Christmas off to be with Luca. They'd had a good time, but he had so much energy, a trip to a lake house might be just the solution. He could get out into the sunshine and run around, breathe in the fresh air and just be a little boy. Sometimes, he was just too smart for his age. She worried that he was growing up too quickly.

"I suppose I could take a break," she said, tapping her pencil against her desk as she tried to think of all the things she'd have to coordinate in order to get out of town quickly.

Marcia stood up and pulled something out of her pocket. "I'm glad that you are accepting my offer this time because I was going to kick you out of here anyway. You're officially on vacation right now," she said, dumping a set of keys onto Callie's desk. "I don't want to see you back here, for any reason, until next Monday."

Callie opened her mouth to protest but Marcia was almost out of the doorway but she stopped and lifted her hand into the air, silencing Callie's protests before she could even start. "I'm not kidding Callie," Marcia warned with the "evil eye" her boss and friend had perfected over the years. "Get out of here. I'll even let Laura take over your job while you're gone. You've been telling me she needs more responsibility for months so now is her chance, unless you take it away from her."

Callie snapped her mouth shut and glared at her boss. "You don't play fair, Marcia." But a moment later, her expression cleared up and she smiled brightly. "But you're a wonderful person, so I'll forgive you." She was almost dancing in her excitement and relief to get out of town, to avoid Zahir, which was really the only way she was going to stay out of his arms. He was just that lethal to her willpower.

Marcia hmphed. "You don't know how evil I can be. If you don't show up at my parents' lake house by lunch time, I'll bring back ten more projects from the Erinson Company."

Callie gasped at that threat. The Erinson Company was a nightmare to work for. Callie worked for FabWebDesigns and normally she loved producing designs for the various clients, trying to figure out how they wanted their websites to look and feel, the main purpose of their needs and giving it to them. It was a dream job that had saved her both physically and psychologically after she came back from Larcatia and the horrible events there.

Besides, Marcia was the most amazing boss. When Callie had first started working here, it had only been the two of them. Callie had heard about the job accidentally and submitted her resume, had an interview with Marcia the following morning and was working on designs by that afternoon. Marcia had given her a chance when she'd been a complete mess, trying to mentally and physically recover from a nightmarish period in her life. At the time, she hadn't even known that she was pregnant with Luca but, when Callie had discovered her pregnancy, Marcia had been there all the way, almost like a grandmother, excited and protective throughout the whole pregnancy.

The Erinson Company was just one of those clients that could never be satisfied. They demanded more graphics and complicated web designs, requesting schemes outside the scope of what the design team would normally take on. On the one hand, they'd challenged Callie to learn more, to work harder and, in the end, the Erinson Company had praised her work. But it had been a challenge that she didn't necessarily want to endure again. Clients like that were miserable to work with.

So when threatened with more projects from that company, she gave in without further argument. "I'll go!" she laughed, raising her hands in surrender. "Let me just finish up what I'm doing and I'll leave Saturday morning."

Marcia immediately shook her head. "No. Take off now. I know there's nothing urgent on your task list right now so go, pack up Luca's stuff while he's still at Ms. Fisher's house," she said, referring to the amazing woman who lived across the hall from Callie and loved watching Luca during the day. Ms. Fisher was like the grandmother she'd never had with a loving hand and a penchant for making the most delicious cookies. Callie's hand moved to her stomach, thinking that she needed to cut back on some of the cookies.

Marcia immediately noticed the self-conscious gesture and laughed. "Don't even try to tell me you're getting fat," Marcia teased. "If anything, you've lost weight and could stand to put on a few pounds. Oh, what I could have done twenty years ago with looks like yours," she laughed. "I could have snagged a king." Marcia laughed at her joke as she turned and walked out of the office, supposedly heading to her own domain. She had no idea the impact her words had on Callie.

Callie tried to pick up the keys, pretend that Marcia's words were just a fluke, but her hands were shaking and her stomach suddenly felt like it wanted to empty the protein bar and apple she'd eaten for breakfast.

Would it always be like this? Even a casual reference to her past and she was trembling so badly she couldn't even stand up. Oh, if Zahir could see her now, his black eyes would crinkle in the corners, the only sign of his amusement. And then he would…

She gasped as the impact of what he would do seized her and she shook her head, taking several deep breaths to try and calm herself down. Bending over, she took great, heaping gulps of air, trying to banish the image of Zahir from her mind.

"So…" Laura popped back into Callie's office and Callie swung her head back up, staring at her friend with wide, nervous eyes. "Are you okay?"

Laura looked at Callie across her desk and rushed in, setting her coffee cup down on the corner of the desk to hurry around to the other side. "What's wrong? What just happened?"

Callie fought back the tears and Laura's protective instincts kicked in. This beautiful woman seemed to be sad more often than not. And Laura had no idea why. Men in restaurants stumbled over themselves when Callie passed by, conversations stopped and women's eyes narrowed with jealousy. Even Laura would hate Callie if she weren't so kind and sweet on the inside. Never had lived a more generous person than Callie and Laura was now worried about her best friend.

Callie raised her hand, trying to assure Laura that she was okay. But her hand was trembling and she tucked it back on her lap. "I'm fine," she said, trying to actually be okay.

"What happened?" Laura asked again, this time more gently, but with a tone that spoke volumes.

There was no way Callie could explain. It was silly really, but just the mention, the mere reference to Zahir always sent her mind spinning out of control, not to mention her body's silly, crazy reaction. The actual man, if he could be called a mere man, had a much more substantial impact on her senses. Goodness, she had to get over him! It had been almost five years! She was twenty-six now! She should be more mature, less crazed when his name came up.

"The dragon lady said something to you, didn't she?" Laura took Callie's hand, trying to rub some warmth into her freezing fingers. "I promise you, her bark is worse than her bite. She's really an old softy inside so whatever happened..."

Callie laughed and shook her head, reassured that Laura understood that Marcia wasn't really so bad. "No. I'm fine, really." And she would be fine! Darn it, she would be perfectly fine. "In fact, she insisted that I take a vacation."

Laura's smile brightened. "Good! You need one. You've been working way too hard."

Callie laughed as she rolled her eyes with Laura's agreement. "I was out of here before you last night," she countered.

Laura shrugged. "Yeah, well, I guess I'm just a sucker for a cute guy. I spoke to the client last night and he sounds really hot. So I'm trying to impress him a little."

Callie could definitely understand that. "Yeah, we need to find some nice, available men, don't we?" Callie refused to think of Zahir as "available". The man was not available or even a nice guy. He was totally off limits.

She sat up and took a few more deep breaths. "I'll be out of town at Lake Anna for a week. But when I get back, let's just make it a plan to find some hot, interesting men for the two of us. We'll make it a mission."

Marcia stepped in and took the file back that she'd given to Callie earlier. "That sounds like a much better plan than doing the online dating thing," she told the two women. "Laura, you're in charge of the team starting now since," she turned to glower at Callie, "your supervisor is leaving for a well-earned vacation."

And again Marcia walked out the door.

Laura turned, her eyes wide with surprise and excitement at their boss' words. A moment later, she yelped with delight as she turned and gave Callie a huge hug. "You did this, didn't you? Old Dragon Lady is finally giving me a chance and it's all because of you."

Callie hugged Laura back but shook her head. "No, Laura, it's because you're a hard worker and you're really good at your job."

Laura jumped up and down with excitement. "Okay, I know you're lying but go, get out of here so I can prove myself. Old Dragon Lady is giving me a chance and I'm going to shine!" Laura danced out of the office, apparently thrilled with her new responsibilities, even if they were only temporary.

Callie laughed, excited for her lovely friend. She and Laura hit the gym during their lunch breaks as often as possible, which generally meant only about three afternoons a week. But she and Laura had a lot in common. Well, Laura didn't have a rambunctious, adorable four year old, but they were both single, both loved computers and design work and Callie loved Laura's mind. The woman really was a genius when it came to inspiring design work. Callie knew that their work environment didn't help their dating status. The two of them really needed to get out and socialize more, meet men or at least other women who might know normal men.

Laura popped her head back into the office just as Callie was picking up the keys from the desk. "If that sexy delivery guy comes in, the one who has been hot for you for the past six months, I'm going to tell him that you're not only available, but you'll meet him for a drink next week."

Callie opened her mouth to object, but Laura was already out the door. And really, what was the harm? Callie truly did need to get out and meet men. Luca was growing up so fast and he needed a man's influence. She was doing her best, but he constantly asked about his father, wanted to learn to fish and camp, things Callie had no clue how to do, nor did she have any desire to do. She'd had one grueling experience 'roughing it'. She would never, ever subject herself to that again.

She was packing up her bag, stuffing a few work things in that she could finish up tonight after Luca was tucked into bed. Callie had to be fair about this camping stuff. Her experience hadn't been camping. It had been….well, it had been a nightmare and camping was supposed to be fun. She shuddered at the idea of being around bugs and worms and creepy crawly things. She hated bugs after her experience, totally lost it when a spider crawled into her apartment. The first time it had happened, she'd totally freaked out, running out of her apartment screaming. If it hadn't been for her sweet building maintenance guy coming to her rescue, she might have been institutionalized that night. As it was, she was standing out in her hallway screeching with Luca in her arms. He'd been just a baby at the time, but her screeching had woken him up, as well as the other tenants on the floor. All of them had tried to help her calm down but it had been Mike, the maintenance guy who had stormed into her place, bat in one hand and a grim expression on his face as he tried to figure out what was going on.

When she'd told him that there'd been a spider, everyone on the floor had looked at her as if she were a crazy female that needed valium. All except for Mike who simply walked back into her apartment, found the spider and killed it.

Ms. Fisher had let her stay in her spare bedroom that night. Mike had ensured that someone came to spray for bugs the next day and several of the other tenants had teased her for her sleepwear over the next few weeks. To them, it had all been a hilarious night but for Callie, it had been traumatizing.

She picked up her bag and the keys, ready to head out of the office, eager now to start a real vacation. It suddenly occurred to her that Mike was always close by, fixing things in the other apartments on her floor. She was thinking it was strange that the building always felt so empty now. One by one, the tenants had moved out of the building. Surely others still lived there now. It wasn't just her and Ms. Fisher, was it? That would be crazy, to have a building with only two tenants?

But she never saw any of the other residents. It was a prime apartment building with great access to the highways, grocery stores and entertainment areas. It wasn't the tallest but it was in a great location just outside of Washington, D.C. in Arlington, Virginia, with extra-large bedrooms, renovated kitchens and great views of the city and the Potomac River. So why didn't she see the other residents? There used to be people coming and going from the front door all the time. But it occurred to her that even the parking lot seemed deserted now. There were cars filling up the lot, but she never saw people coming or going to them. Very odd, she realized.

Chapter 3

Three hours later, after collecting Luca, packing up bags and hitting the grocery store, she pulled her car up and parked it to the side of the driveway, her eyes wide as she took in the magnificent lake house. From this angle, the house was two stories but she could see to the left and right of the enormous house, that there was a third level that was accessible from the back or from the inside. There were so many windows, she wasn't sure how anyone could afford to cool the house down in the summer. Hopefully they were the thermal windows.

She was starting to think that they were at the wrong house when Luca jumped out of the back seat. Her head spun around and she jumped out after him, worried that he might hurt himself in the unknown area.

"Luca, slow down!" she called out as her son sprinted out of the car towards the house. He stopped and looked back at her eagerly, his little body almost shaking with excitement and energy.

"Wanna see the lake!" he called to her, his dark eyes, so similar to his fathers, staring back at her with a pleading look. Okay, so that wasn't like his father, she thought. Zahir had never pleaded with her. He was too alpha male, too dominant. He had never asked, he took. And she'd given! Oh goodness how much she'd given him. Their nights had steamed up the bedroom as he demanded more and more of her, shown her the delights of both his and her body and…she shook her head, trying not to think about him anymore. It was just his return last night that had brought back all of those memories.

Thankfully, she hadn't heard from him again. Hopefully, her sudden absence from work and her apartment would convince him that she couldn't be with him and he'd move on.

Callie looked at the car loaded up with supplies and suitcases, then at the lake visible through the trees. Luca was so excited to be out in the sunshine, why not just let him run? With a sigh, she turned away from the car, not wanting to unload it just yet herself. Her son had the right idea, she thought. "Okay, let's go," she said and almost laughed as the little guy jumped up with eagerness.

"There's a pathway around here, Momma. Let's go!" He was almost around the corner when he looked back at her. With his normal, devilish grin, he sprinted back to her, grabbed her hand then tugged her along with him. "Come on, Momma. Hurry!"

Callie laughed, starting to feel his enthusiasm as the tension of the last day eased out of her. Goodness, Marcia had been right on target. The closer they walked to the lake, the more her strain drifted away. This was good, she thought. They could relax, eat yummy food, she wouldn't worry about her weight this week and they could enjoy the huge batch of cookies Luca and Ms. Fisher had baked up yesterday.

"Hold up, Luca," she called, laughing as he easily skipped down the rock pathway while she had to carefully maneuver her way. "You're smaller so you can do this faster. I'm an old woman with tender feet and I'm definitely not as nimble on these rocks as you are."

Luca was such a sweet little guy. When he realized his mom was having problems, he came right back up to her and grabbed her elbow and hand. He was trying hard to be a gentleman, but his aide was actually making her laugh harder and causing them to slow down more.

Once they'd made it to the long, wooden dock, he dropped her hand, too eager to explore. "Look at all the fish! Can we catch them and have some for dinner?" he exclaimed as he laid is body down on the deck, his head hanging off the edge.

Callie warily looked down from her standing position, not as daring about being close to the elements as her son. There were a bunch of silver fish swimming around, less than an inch in length. "I think those are called feeder fish, honey. The bigger fish eat those and then we catch the bigger fish to eat."

Luca looked up at her, his eyes squinting as he absorbed this information. "So where are the bigger fish?" he asked.

Callie pointed to the deeper water. "I suppose they are out there, waiting for you to jump into the water." She shivered with revulsion at the idea of actually swimming in the murky lake water. Callie hadn't considered that when she'd agreed to this type of a vacation. She supposed she'd have to get into the water. There was no way she'd be able to keep him out of it now that they were here.

She looked into the water warily. Maybe she'd get used to it.

Her eyes skimmed along the shoreline as a truly horrific thought occurred to her. Were there snakes in the woods? Oh goodness, what had she gotten herself into? Of course there were snakes!

Luca was completely oblivious to her snake controversy and jumped up from the dock, not even bothering to dust himself off. He'd investigated the water, ran around the pathway and now, as most young boys his age, he was on to the next thing to investigate. "Where are the cookies?" he asked.

Callie laughed again, relieved to think about something other than bugs and snakes and other creepy things that were in or near lakes. "They're still back in the car. Think you could help me unpack? Bring everything into the house?"

He had already found a rock and was pulling it up, trying to see what was underneath it. But with the promise of cookies in the near future, he let the rock fall back onto the dirt. "Yep!" he said and jumped up onto his feet. "Race you back up!" he said and a moment later, he was zipping back up the hill.

Callie followed at a more leisurely pace, thinking it would be really nice to bottle up his excess energy. She'd had another dream last night so she hadn't slept very well. She'd thought those dreams were fading away, but only one kiss from Zahir and they came right back, just as powerful as before.

Somehow, she'd have to get over him. She couldn't keep doing this to herself.

At least last night's dream wasn't that horrible nightmare she used to have. Those were worse although neither the erotic dreams of being in Zahir's arms nor the nightmarish dreams of being trapped in a dirt pit would allow her to fall back to sleep. Maybe she should see someone about the nightmares. They didn't seem to be fading in intensity. They were just as real now as when they were actually happening.

With a sigh, Callie pushed the issue out of her mind as she rounded the corner of the house once more, thinking this was a pretty isolated house. Just exactly what she needed. It would be a fun week with just her and Luca, swimming in the cove, laughing and cooking whatever they wanted. She ran a hand over her thighs, refusing to think about those extra pounds she'd gained and couldn't seem to get rid of. She didn't have to impress anyone, least of all Luca. He accepted her just the way she was.

Sighing and trying to push the disturbing dreams out of her mind along with all of the other confusing issues, like Zahir and her job, she hurried up the path. This week was going to be simple and easy. Looking up, she realized that she couldn't see Luca any longer. "Hold up, honey. I'll unlock the car."

His sweet face appeared back around the corner of the house. "Mom, the car is gone."

Callie rolled her eyes. "No teasing today, Luca. Mommy's too tired."

"Another dream?" he asked, coming down the pathway and taking her hand.

Callie stopped in her tracks, putting her hand on his head gently. "How did you know?"

The little guy was older than his four years sometimes. "I hear you crying at night sometimes," he explained.

She bent down to his level and hugged him. "I'm sorry, my man. I didn't know that I was waking you up."

He wrapped his arms around her neck and smiled at her. "It's okay. I'm going to grow big and strong and I'll protect you. Once I'm bigger, you won't have the nightmares any longer." He turned serious again as he said, "But the car really is gone."

She still thought he was teasing. He loved playing pranks on her and she squeezed his back slightly. "Of course."

Callie stood up and took his hand as they walked the short distance to the driveway. When they turned the corner of the house, she stopped cold. Her car was gone! Her car with everything in it. All their clothes, food for the week, her purse, credit cards…her phone…everything!

"Where's the car?" she gasped, trying to think back. Had she parked it somewhere else? Did they walk up to the wrong house? Callie spun around, trying to find the car but it was pretty hard to hide a vehicle. It sort of stood out so it wasn't like someone could be playing hide and seek in the woods with her car.

Even the keys to the house were in the car!

"Oh no!" she whispered to herself, trying not to let Luca know how panicked she was. Phone! She needed to get to a phone and call the police.

"We can go inside Momma," Luca was saying, tugging at her hand. "Why don't we just call Mike? He always knows what to do and how to fix things."

Callie followed behind him simply because she was so stunned that she'd stupidly left everything in her car. Now her son was at risk and they were stuck in the forest with no one close by. But she knew there were other houses. This was Lake Anna. There were houses everywhere along the waterfront and even complete neighborhoods.

When that thought struck her, she started to breathe a bit easier. Sure, it would be a hassle, but they could walk a bit and find someone who could help….

"See? The door's already open." Luca walked into the house and whooped it up. "Wow! Momma, come see! This place is huge!"

Callie forced herself to step into the cool, dark interior of the house, immediately grateful for the air conditioning. Why would Marcia's parents leave the house unlocked? That seemed extremely strange. But she wasn't going to look a gift horse in the mouth. She entered and looked around for a phone. She had to call the police, fast! Maybe whoever had stolen her car could be stopped before they got too far away.

"Okay, honey. I'll come and look, I just need to make a quick phone call."

She picked up the phone and started dialing but something…she couldn't put her finger on it but there was a tension in the air. Callie looked around the house, her senses suddenly on high alert.

Something was wrong!

"Luca, come here, sweety," she called out. Luca looked back at her with a question in his eyes. "Just come over here, love. I need to…"

"Hello Callie," a deep voice said from behind her.

Callie's hand gripped the phone and the blood drained from her face. That voice! No, it couldn't be! Please, don't let it be him! Of all the people in the world, please don't let him be standing behind her again! She'd come all the way out here to avoid this man! How could he be standing right behind her?

"You look good," that voice said and there was no way she could ignore that sensation any longer. Spinning around, the phone fell from her nerveless fingers and she gripped the edge of the table. Breathing was a luxury as the extremely tall man from her past came out of the shadows just as he had in her apartment so recently. Her first thought was that he looked better than good in the casual clothes. He looked…amazing! She'd never seen him in casual, only a suit or…well, naked.

His eyes practically singed her skin as they traveled from her blond hair down to her toes, hesitating at her breasts that were pressing up against the tee-shirt that was too small after so many washings not to mention nursing a hungry baby for twelve months.

He came closer and her body tingled, her nostrils flared, trying desperately to catch his scent. But she was too confused and her knees were shaking so badly, surely he could see them giving way.

"You can't be here," she whispered. "It's impossible."

"And yet, here I am," he retorted, lifting his war roughened hand to caress her cheek gently.

With those words and his touch, Callie lost it. Perhaps it was her fitful sleep or the terror of her car being stolen, putting Luca at risk. Or maybe it was just this man standing in front of her after she'd come all this way to avoid him. But she lost it. The world simply blacked out and she felt herself falling. And then nothing.

Chapter 4

Zahir looked down at the beautiful woman lying on the bed, her blond hair floating out against the pillow and her long, dark lashes laying against her pale skin. The guards and Ms. Fisher were caring for his son but Zahir watched the woman, feeling guilty for the scare he'd given her that had caused this. He shouldn't have sprung everything on her so quickly. He should have been more cautious. After seeing her last night in her apartment, he should have warned her that he would be here.

Of course, if she'd had any warning, she probably would not have come. Which was why he'd come up with this surprise plan in the first place.

"She'll be fine," the doctor said as he stood up from the bed. "Just a faint," he assured Zahir. "She's coming around now."

The doctor closed his case and nodded to Zahir who didn't acknowledge the man in any way other than a slight nod. His eyes were staring, trying to find signs of life in the prone woman on the bed, willing her to recover. He'd spent so much time apart from her. It had been necessary, but things were finally in place. He'd gotten his country back in order and now it was time for Callie to take her place by his side. And in his bed.

Damn, she looked lovely. She was healthier now. Well, except for the fact that she was passed out from fear of him. The other night, he hadn't had the time to take his fill of her golden beauty but now, with her lying still on the bed, he could let his eyes roam over her lushes curves and her long legs. He just wished she were awake, that he hadn't scared her into a dead faint.

She'd get over that fear, he told himself. He would take things slowly, make sure she was comfortable with the changes that were going to happen to her and then explain everything.

Callie turned her head, her mind still fuzzy but flashes of the day slowly came back to her. When she opened her eyes, she instantly knew that something was wrong. This wasn't her room. This room was too big, too luxurious.

When she lifted her head to look around, she tried to get her bearings but everything inside of her was clenching because she knew that this was wrong.

When she found Zahir, he was standing at the foot of the bed, his arms crossed over his chest as he glared down at her.

"It was you," she whispered, her throat dry and the panic coming right back to her. "Go away," she whispered. "I told you yesterday that I don't want you here." She ignored that tightness, the almost painful anticipation lower in her belly that she felt every time Zahir looked at her.

She was not going down that road again, she told herself firmly. She would not do this to herself or to Luca. Zahir made her lose control. He could do it with a look, a simple touch or just walking into a room. It was so unfair that he had that kind of power over her but she had to pretend otherwise.

She was unaware that her nipples were pressing against the thin cotton of her tee-shirt or that her body had already turned towards his, giving him all the information he needed.

"Go away, Zahir. You're not wanted here."

He didn't go away, not even to leave the room. In fact, his only response was to laugh softly at her command, leaving his handsome features with amusement curling those lips that....

Ugh! Callie refused to remember what those lips could do.

"You're not listening to me, Zahir. I don't love you anymore. I won't ever love you. We couldn't make it work before and I don't care if you say that the war is over. I don't believe it. Come back in another five years," she told him as she swung her legs off of the side of the bed and stood up. "If you can maintain peace between the countries for five years, then I'll believe that the peace will last."

Again, he didn't respond. But his eyes moved over her figure, his lips smiling as he listened to her words that were a blatant challenge to his authority.

That smile curled her toes. He was so raw, so savage. Everything about him spoke of that barely leashed power that was all Zahir. She had no idea what it was about him but she just turned to mush when those black eyes looked in her direction. The skin on his face had pulled tighter over his high cheekbones, indicating he'd lost weight over the past five years. But his upper body was bigger, his muscles bulging through the tight cotton shirt he wore. His stomach had always been flat but now, with those casual slacks belted around his hips, riding lower than she remembered, his stomach looked...tight. Drawn almost which was ridiculous because she couldn't see his stomach. It was just the impression of him. Everything about him was...savage.

There was no other word to use. The man was brutally strong, capable of the most astounding gentleness but she knew firsthand what the man was up against with his country at war and the ravages of countless battles. The inhuman brutality of war was what this man had lived through for more than a decade. He'd lost both of his parents to that war. And he'd lost her. She'd met Zahir while she'd been waitressing in college and had fallen head over heels for him. After knowing him for less than a week, she'd gone with him back to his country, been so in love with him that she'd simply pushed the far off war out of her consciousness. It didn't affect her so she refused to acknowledge it.

But then it had affected her. In the most personal way, it had affected her and she could never go back, could never risk Luca's life or his happiness by going back.

So no matter how much her body yearned to feel that sexual pull that Zahir wove around her, she couldn't do it. She was a mother now. Callie couldn't take those risks.

"This isn't your house. You have to leave."

She pushed herself away from the bed, not wanting to be so close to the flat surface. Beds were dangerous because of their usefulness at what he was an expert at doing.

She noticed his look and stepped further away. "Don't!" she snapped at him.

Of course, he ignored her order, his hands taking hers and pulling her closer. Right into his arms. "Let me go, Zahir!" she said, wishing her voice didn't quiver or that her body didn't almost fall against his hard, muscular frame. She curled her fingers into a fist, refusing to let her fingertips explore.

"You have gained weight," he said, his voice a grumbling sound that lifted all the hairs on her skin to full awareness of this man.

She pushed against him but his hands only moved down lower, sliding along her body to rest against her back. "I like it. The weight makes you softer. More lovely than before. You were too thin five years ago."

She was horrified to feel that betraying tightening even more with his words. "No!" she said harshly. "I won't let you pull me into your life again."

His eyes moved over her lovely features, taking in all the changes that five years would do to a woman's face and he knew that she was even more beautiful now. "I'm afraid it is time to come home, Callie."

She trembled but shook her head. "I'm on vacation, Zahir. And next week, I will go home. To my own home and not to yours. I promised I would never set foot in Larcatia after…" she couldn't finish the sentence. "Well, after all that happened. And I'm not going back on my word."

His hand smoothed up her back and he almost laughed with relief when she arched into him. Yes, she was still his woman. Even after all these years, his Callie reacted to his touch the same way.

"I told you, the war is over."

Her body froze with those words. "And I told you that I don't believe it. It can't be over. It is never really over. It is more likely that the problems underlying all the hostilities are just simmering and who knows what could fan the sparks back to a raging war."

He shook his head slowly, his dark, almost black eyes watching her carefully, feasting on her delicate beauty. "No. That's not going to happen. The war is over. Peace is everywhere. Every citizen is working to maintain that peace and I will make it last."

"How can you be sure?" she whispered, her heart heavy with the news. Joyous yes, but also heavy with the knowledge that thousands, possibly hundreds of thousands of people had died in the conflict that had lasted for so long.

"I am sure. I meet with the leaders of Tularia, Lurasa and Altair regularly. It has been six months since a shot has been fired. The people are accepting this peace. They are desperate for it, in fact. As I told you the other night, everyone is trying to re-build their lives. What you don't know is that we are working to build understanding between the four countries, to sponsor events that will draw people from the previously warring countries as well as other cultures to show everyone that we're finished with the fighting."

Callie so desperately wanted to believe his words, but she wasn't going to. But nor was she going to shoot down his hopes and dreams. "That's really wonderful news, Zahir. I'm so happy for you." He must have worked very hard to get all of this in place. She sincerely hoped it would work out, for him and for everyone.

"So you will come home. You will rule with me," his hand drifted into her hair, tangling in the soft, spun gold. "You will be my queen and we'll grow the country." With his last word, his lips touched hers. He didn't wait for her agreement, just took her lips and kissed her as if five years hadn't just separated them. It was the gentlest kiss he'd ever given to her. Even the first time he'd kissed her, it had been overwhelming. But this kiss, this gentle caress, made her whimper for more. For something deeper. Stronger.

And he gave it to her. Zahir had always given her exactly what she wanted even though, most times, she didn't know she wanted it. Or even those times she was too embarrassed to ask for it, he knew. It was as if he could read her mind and she'd thrilled to everything he'd taught her about her body and sexuality during their tempestuous three weeks together.

When her fists opened up and grabbed onto the cotton of his shirt, he instantly deepened the kiss, giving to her what she was silently begging him to do. She had no idea how he could understand her so perfectly, but at this moment, as his hand moved up to cup her jaw, opening her mouth so that his tongue could invade her mouth, she didn't care. Her body involuntarily pressed against his, shifting her breasts to create that friction that she craved more than food or water.

The feeling of his rough hands against her bare skin startled her out of the sensual haze that had wrapped her mind in cotton gauze, pulling her back to reality with a thud. "No!" she gasped and wrenched herself out of his arms.

The only reason he released her was because he was surprised. The look in his eyes told her that much but she knew that she wasn't free.

Her shaking fingers reached up and touched her lips, still feeling like she was on fire. Sure enough, her lips were swollen. Just one kiss from him and she was back in his clutches.

"No," she whispered. "I won't let you do this to me again. I'm not that same person I used to be. I've grown up and I'm smarter now."

Zahir watched her carefully, wondering where she was going with this discussion. "And what have your years of wisdom taught you?" he asked, amused but still so hard and aching to have her back in his arms that he might just start howling. Slowly, he reminded himself. Slow and steady. Eventually, she would be his. He had to approach her strategically. She was hurt and scared but he would win her over.

She pulled her shirt down lower, still unaware of those nipples that contradicted everything she was saying. "I don't want you anymore Zahir. I learned my lesson the last time we were together. I can't live in your world. And I know you can't give up your country to come to mine. So we'll just have to go our separate ways."

"There are a few problems with your logic, my beauty," he said, crossing his arms over his chest. His eyes kept dropping to her breasts, wanting to explore those nipples, to suckle them again and see her come apart for him. He remembered how sensitive those nipples were, how she could almost climax when he teased them just so. And now she was standing five feet away from him, those nipples begging him to treat them to his expert touch.

Callie realized what he was looking at and wrapped her arms across her chest, glaring back at him defiantly. "And what's that?" she demanded.

"You're my wife," he said softly.

His words, spoken with such conviction and victory, sounded through the room like a dead weight. She stared at him, her body going cold, then hot as she waited for him to laugh and tell her that he was just kidding.

"No," she whispered back, trying to gain sound but her voice simply refused to work. "No," she shook her head. "We were engaged. You proposed, I accepted, we flew to your country and we were going to be married. But then I was…I mean," she looked down, then back up to his eyes again, "I am not your wife."

"We were married. Two days after your return from that demented man's clutches and before I would let you out of my sight, we were married."

Her mind flashed back again. She'd been so scared and angry after…

She shook her head. "No. I told you I was going home and you agreed."

"I agreed because I finally understood the danger you were in. But no, my beauty. We were married the day you got onto the plane."

She tried to think back to that horrible time. She'd been so scared after…but there were those few minutes, in the basement of the palace. "When we were in that room," she croaked out through stiff lips. "The room with all the frescos. It was so pretty and you held my hands. I knew you were trying to tell me something but I couldn't listen. I was still so traumatized by the…"

"The man talking beside us married us quickly. Before you got on the plane."

She shook her head. "But I never agreed! I didn't agree to become your wife!"

He walked over to her, his hand smoothing back the golden locks that floated about her face as the air conditioner worked to cool down the house from the August heat. "You gave your consent when you agreed to marry me. In Larcatia, that is a committment."

She couldn't believe what he was saying. It was impossible! "That's barbaric!" she cried out. "And completely irrelevant. I didn't give my consent, I didn't agree. Therefore, we're not married."

He chuckled. "I assure you, we are legally married. Just because you don't agree with the laws, doesn't mean they don't apply to you."

She jerked back but cringed when she discovered that his fingers were tangled in her hair. "Well, then, I'll just get a divorce!" She lifted her hands, unaware that the movement pressed her breasts against the thin cotton of her tee-shirt again. She quickly disentangled his fingers from her hair and glared up at him.

He laughed softly again with her attempt at being stern. She was so soft and her hair was so beautiful, her glares only made her look more sensuous, a fact that he was definitely not going to tell her at this moment. "That is indeed a woman's choice."

She huffed and stepped away from him. "I'm so glad that women have some legal standing in your country."

He shrugged one massive shoulder. "You must prove abuse or infidelity to obtain a divorce."

Her mouth fell open with that bombshell. "I haven't seen you in almost five years! How am I to prove how many women you've slept with over the years?"

He shook his head. "Then I supposed we will remain married," he told her with wicked intent in those dangerously dark eyes.

Those words stirred something deep inside of her, something she didn't understand nor would she examine too closely. She couldn't because that horrible excitement could hurt her. Badly!

"No. That simply isn't going to happen, Zahir," she declared, not even wanting to think of any other woman touching this man's body or of his mouth doing…. Zahir was a passionate man. During the weeks they'd been together, they had spent a great deal of that time in bed, exploring each other's bodies. And boy, did he know how to make her scream with need! He'd been intoxicating and infuriating

32

and everything inside of her clenched at the memories of the power he'd had over her.

"You're remembering all of the nights and days we spent in bed, aren't you?"

She stepped back once again, taking a deep breath. "We have nothing between us, Zahir. We're just two people who tried and failed."

He shook his head, his eyes conveying the finality of his next words. "Callie, you are my wife. We have five years of marriage between us and a son. A boy who is amazing and I thank you for caring for our son so well."

Callie felt like a steel band was wrapping around her chest. How did he know about Luca? She'd been so careful! "You stay away from Luca," she gasped. "He's my son! You can't have him! I refuse to let you take him back to that country where humans can do such…horrific acts to another human being. I won't let you, Zahir. I'll fight you."

"Since you are my wife, there is little chance of a legal battle being successful, my dear."

Callie heard his words and the panic went higher. Was he right? Could he take Luca away from her? The idea of never seeing her little boy again made her stomach feel nauseous. "I can still divorce you. There has to be a way."

He chuckled and moved closer. "Yes. There are other ways. Perhaps you could prove that you no longer feel the same way you did during the wedding."

She grasped onto that. "Well, since I was terrified out of my mind, that should be easy enough to prove."

"If both parties agree to a divorce, it is a simple matter of dissolving the marriage." With that, he bent lower and kissed her neck, enjoying the way she shivered and tried to pull away, but her body couldn't do it.

"I would ask you for a divorce," she said, shuddering and taking another step backwards, "but I doubt you're going to be reasonable about this."

"Not a chance," he agreed. "So I guess we're stuck with each other."

She shook her head. "I can get a divorce here in the US. I'll figure out a way." She once again stepped around him and walked to the other side of the bed. "I have to take care of my son and you have to get out of this house. It isn't yours, it isn't even mine. So just…"

She stopped in her tracks and looked around. "Where is Luca?"

Zahir quickly saw the panic develop in her pretty amber eyes and stepped in to help her ease the concern. "He is safe. Ms. Fisher arrived right after you fainted and she has been watching over him. Also, my guards have been teaching him to fish down at the dock so have no fear. They will protect him with their lives."

She took a deep breath and pushed her hair out of her eyes. "Great," she sighed. "No problem. My son is surrounded by men with guns down by the water."

He looked at her curiously, trying to understand her. "What concerns you the most?" he asked. "The fact that our son is safe without you? Or that he's with my men? Men that he will someday rule, I have to point out."

Callie didn't like the sound of that at all. Luca was never going to that horrible country! It might be beautiful and amazing but it was also devastated by a horrible war. "No. He is just a little boy. You can't determine his whole future when he's just four years old."

He took her hand and tucked it onto his arm. "Callie, his future was decided the moment he was conceived. I'm sorry that this disturbs you, but I will ensure that he is trained well to take his place as ruler of Larcatia." He opened the door and led her out into the lovely house that had enormous windows that looked out onto the lake where the sun was sparkling in the late afternoon sunshine. "And we will have more children that will help him rule, will be with him and grow with him."

She shivered at the idea, shaking inside at the possibility of having more children with Zahir. It wasn't the thought of being pregnant again that scared her as much as the process of conception. It had almost killed her to walk away from him the first time. She couldn't let him do that to her again. She might not survive leaving him a second time.

"Zahir, this is..."

She looked out and spotted Luca, laughing up at a big guy that she recognized although, from this distance, she couldn't see him clearly. "Who is that man?" she asked, her voice low and anxious.

Zahir looked down to the dock and smiled with pride. The boy was already strong and confident. He would make a good leader. "His name is Amman."

"I've seen him before! He works in the building I live in. I thought he worked for Mike."

"Who is Mike?" Zahir asked, a tinge of anger tainting his voice.

Callie blinked at his reaction. Was that jealousy? Could he really have strong feelings for her? She hesitated, not sure what to think.

Zahir could barely contain his fury when his wife uttered another man's name so casually. "Callie, answer the damn question. Who the hell is Mike?" he demanded once again, turning so that they were facing each other.

Callie started to think that this might be a good idea. If he was jealous, maybe he would let her go. Maybe he would think she was tainted. Zahir was a possessive man. And old-fashioned. He wouldn't want her if she'd slept with another man, would he?

She smiled victoriously, feeling only a slight twinge of guilt at the deceitful implications she was about to give Zahir. "Mike is a really great guy," she told him, staying within truth's boundaries but omitting pertinent details that weren't useful to her.

"And what is he to you?" he demanded. Zahir looked into her golden eyes and felt more fury than he'd thought possible. He couldn't believe that his guards hadn't protected her. He would have words with Marcia and the rest of them, demanding to know how a man had gotten through their protective layers.

Callie's chin went up. "Like I said, he's a nice guy. He comes over and helps me whenever I call on him for any reason. He's polite and kind and I know that I'm safe when he's around."

Zahir thought his mind might explode at the possibility of another man being in her apartment. It was impossible! He'd gotten reports on her activities almost daily! How could his men have omitted a man entering her apartment? And it sounded like this was an ongoing event!

"Tell me what I need to hear, Callie!" he growled, ready to do physical harm to this man. "I want his name. I want his full name and I want to know where he lives."

Callie cringed, feeling awful but she pushed that feeling aside. This was her life she was dealing with. She couldn't back down. This was too important.

"I won't let you hurt him, Zahir."

He ignored the worry in her pretty, amber eyes, his entire focus on getting the name of the man who had dared to touch his wife. "I'll rip him apart, just as soon as I get the information I need."

She pulled out of his arms and backed up. "Then I'm not telling you anything."

Zahir barked an order in his own language. Immediately, a man stepped into the room, startling Callie who had thought they were alone. "Where did…?"

Zahir ignored her and spoke in the same language, obviously demanding to know who had entered Callie's apartment. But this man…did he look familiar too? Was she losing her mind?

The man quickly responded in the same language, gesturing slightly. When he backed up with a bow, Zahir turned back to Callie with a triumphant gleam in his eyes. "Mike is one of my men, Callie. His real name is Haffas Ilarasas and he has been in my employ for the past fifteen years."

Callie's mouth dropped open as the implication of what he was saying hit her. "He works for you?" she asked with a sinking feeling in the pit of her stomach.

"Yes." Zahir twirled her around so that she was once again in his arms. "So you see, my little liar, your 'Mike' is no one that could make me jealous, but I appreciate the reason you tried."

Callie couldn't believe what she was hearing. "Leave me alone," she grumbled, trying to push him away again. "I'm going to start my vacation and, when I get back up to start dinner, you'd better be out of here. I want to have this time with my son all alone."

Callie didn't wait for him to respond. She simply opened the sliding glass doors and walked down the stairs of the elaborate deck that wrapped around the back side of the house. She was fuming inside, feeling like a fool but that was her fault. She never should have tried to challenge Zahir. He was better at all the games and made up his own rules while she played by the ones she thought were set in stone.

"I'll take over now," she said to the man as politely as possible. It was hard because she knew that this man was here specifically to guard the boy who might become a future ruler unless Callie was very smart and very careful.

When the man walked back up into the woods, apparently leaving them alone on the dock, she breathed a bit easier. "What are you doing?" she asked.

Luca's grin lightened her heart, as it always did. "I'm fishin'" he exclaimed and handed her the fishing rod that the guard had abandoned a moment ago. "You can bait the hook with the worms over there," he told her, pointing to a plastic container that looked as if it only contained dirt. She guessed that this was only a pretend fishing expedition and was grateful to the guard who hadn't given her four-year-old son a real hook. Those things had always freaked her out. "Okay, sounds like a plan." She sat down next to him, letting her feet dangle over the edge of the deck, grateful that the deck was high enough that her feet weren't in the water. "What are we fishing for?" She figured she could ease herself closer and closer to the murky depths of the lake, getting used to not seeing what was around her. There was absolutely no way she was going to touch the bottom though! Nope, that was out of the question. How she was going to accomplish that…well, she'd need to work on that part of her plan. She cringed at the very idea of her toes touching the muddy bottom of the lake. Ick! "Are there even any fish around here?" she asked, peering down carefully.

Luca looked out at the water. "Catfish!" He tugged his fishing pole slightly, obviously working very hard to concentrate on his fishing skills. "You have to be really quiet," he explained in a stage whisper, "because voices scare the fish away."

"Ah," she replied, her feet swaying back and forth. She wanted very badly to look back up at the house, to see if Zahir was leaving. He wouldn't, she thought with rising desperation. The sun was setting slowly but Zahir was still in the house. What was she going to do if he wasn't gone by the time Luca needed to get ready for bed? She couldn't sleep in the same house with him. She just couldn't!

"You okay, momma?" he asked, forgetting his whisper voice.

"I'm fine, buddy. Why do you ask?" She ruffled his hair, thinking he needed a haircut. Again!

"You just moaned like you were in pain." He went back to concentrating on his fishing. "You do that a lot at night too."

Callie blushed, shocked that her son had heard her during her dreams. She was really going to have to get some sort of soundproofing for her room. "I think I'm just hungry."

He nodded his head. "You should stop dieting," he told her with the same stern expression that his father tended to use. "You look pretty just the way you are."

Callie's heart melted for her little son. She'd tried to hide her attempts to lose weight from him, not wanting him to have the same self-image issues she had. But there was a difference between males and females. Her mind flashed back to Zahir who was most likely NOT gathering his things to leave. Zahir didn't have any self-confidence issues. Another point in his favor and her heart wrenched with the realization that Luca definitely needed Zahir's presence in his life.

Luca lifted his fishing pole out of the water with a heartfelt sigh. "Lost another one," he grumbled. "Okay momma, it's your turn. You gotta put the worm on the hook."

Callie was more than willing to play along. "A worm, eh?" she offered, looking at the hook. "That looks like a real hook, honey," she said with concern. Hooks could get into little hands and hurt them. "I'm not sure if I like this game."

Luca rolled his eyes. "I'm really fishin' Momma. And you've gotta put the worm on the hook. Just dig in that cup and get one out. They don't bite."

Callie looked over at the plastic cup again. Picking it up, she wondered why he thought there were worms in here.

And then the dirt moved. She didn't believe her eyes initially but when it moved again, her heart stopped beating. With a scream, she tossed the cup of worms into the air and scrambled backwards, anywhere that took her away from the cup of moving dirt. She couldn't seem to stop screaming even though she could hear Luca laughing at how silly she was being.

A moment later, strong arms were lifting her up, cradling her and Zahir's deep voice was soothing her. "It's okay, love. No one is here to hurt you. I won't let that happen again. I promise."

Callie heard his voice, knew that she'd overreacted, again, but she couldn't get her arms to loosen from around his neck. She wanted to wrap her whole body around him, to absorb his strength.

Callie knew that she could handle almost anything that fate threw her way but bugs, and now worms, were not one of them. She hadn't minded bugs when she was a kid. It was only after three days and nights of being held in a hole, where bugs crawled out of the dirt and she was trapped with no one to hear her screams, that she had developed a phobia about bugs. And worms.

Long minutes passed and she still held onto him. She heard Zahir speaking to Luca in the background and her little traitor was telling his newfound father about how freaked out Callie gets when a spider or bug gets into the house. "Yeah, Mike makes sure that the bug guy comes around a lot to spray for bugs. She's okay around flies now, but boy, you should have seen her last summer."

Callie's shaking was now only occasional trembles as she listened to her son explain her phobia of bugs and anything creepy crawly. The little guy had no idea!

"Hey," Zahir said, pulling away just slightly so he could look at her face. "You okay?' he asked.

Callie nodded, prying her hands away from his neck slowly. "Yes. I'm fine," she said and cleared her throat. "Sorry about that." Her voice sounded raw after that screaming, she realized.

He wasn't convinced and put a hand on her hips, holding her in position on his lap. "Don't go away too soon. Jabril is hooking the worm now, so don't look over there."

Callie shuddered and once more buried her face in Zahir's neck, inhaling his clean, citrus and male scent. "Tell me when it is over," she pleaded, gripping his shirt and wiggling closer to him.

Zahir glanced over, not sure if he wanted the activity to go on or stop. Callie was in his arms and her wiggling against his body was making him harden with the pleasure of her softness once again close to him. But that wiggling was also pure torture because he couldn't do anything about it. Not with his son so near.

He satisfied himself with putting his hands on her soft, round bottom and holding her close, enjoying her gentle, sweet breath against his neck.

Luca was watching closely, he noticed.

"You're touching my momma," he said, his eyes narrowing and his little body was stiff with a latent protectiveness she'd never seen before.

Zahir looked over Callie's shoulder but wouldn't release her. "Yes. You're right. You're Luca." He didn't ask either. He obviously knew all about his son and her whole body stiffened with reaction. She wanted to deny the truth, to hide Luca away so that Zahir couldn't steal her son, but the truth was, he had every right to know Luca and the amazing little boy that he was. And she hated that truth!

"Stay away from him," she whispered in his ear. And she forced her arms to release his neck, not liking her need of his strength. With enormous effort, she stood up and stepped away from him, ignoring the shaking that was still twisting her up inside.

Zahir stood up as well, his eyes hard and unyielding. "It is time, Callie. I will know my son."

Callie stared up at him, her mind whirling, trying to come up with an argument against him. But in the end, her innate sense of fairness wouldn't allow her to hide Luca away from this man. "You won't steal him away from me?" she whispered.

His hand reached up and touched her cheek gently. "Never," he replied.

Her lips trembled for a moment before she pulled herself together. Nodding her head, she looked down, suddenly realizing that Luca had put himself in between herself and Zahir. He was protecting her! She might have thought it was adorable if Zahir hadn't been such an extremely large man.

"Luca," she said, bending lower so that she was at his eye level again, "you know all of those questions you had about your father? About who he was and where he'd gone?"

Luca immediately put two and two together and looked over his shoulder at the tall, dark stranger. "You're my dad?" he asked, awe and excitement in his voice.

Zahir sat back down on the deck chair, looking down at his son. "Yes. And I'm very proud to meet you, Luca," he said, extending his hand carefully for the little guy to shake it.

Luca's eyes lit up just as his face broke out into a beaming smile. "Wow!" he said, putting his smaller hand into Zahir's large, calloused one. "You're my dad!"

Zahir laughed. "And I've been following your progress. I might not have been near, but I always knew what you were up to. Ms. Fisher sent me progress reports every day about what you were learning, what you did, and all the special things that make you my son. So you might not have seen me, but I've been there with you."

Luca still smiled. "You know about the soccer goal I scored last week?" he asked hopefully.

Zahir smiled. "Not only did I know about it, but I saw it! Ms. Fisher sent me the video of your goal and I was proud of how you kicked the ball around those other two players and kicked the ball right into the goal! It was great!"

Callie gasped at this news, shocked that she'd been so oblivious to everything that had been happening to her. "Ms. Fisher is another employee?" she asked, her mind putting the pieces of the puzzle together finally.

Luca nodded his head, his eyes glancing up at Callie and noticing that her arms were crossed over her chest protectively. "She was the nanny I hired as soon as I heard that you were pregnant," he told her.

Callie looked away, wondering what other little secrets he had on her. Had her whole life for the past five years been a game? A fraud? She'd been so proud of her accomplishments, but…she shook her head. There were too many revelations happening. She couldn't keep up with everything.

"Ms. Fisher and I made cookies yesterday. Want to try some?" Luca asked.

Zahir nodded his head somberly. "I think that is the best idea I've heard all day."

Callie followed the two of them as they all walked up the pathway towards the house. There were several pathways – one leading to the front, one leading around the back to the enormous, multi-tiered deck and still others that she hadn't discovered yet.

Luca was talking a mile a minute, trying to fill Zahir in on everything he'd done for the last five years. He was even telling Zahir about his birth, which Callie had told him stories about on his birthday. "And she said she sprinted up the stairs as soon as we came home, just because she could," he said proudly. He shrugged his shoulders. "She didn't like being pregnant, but she likes having me around."

Callie had told him stories about how her legs had been in so much pain during her pregnancy that it had been hard to walk up the stairs. He'd been a larger than average baby and he'd liked to camp out on her sciatic nerve, causing her to have trouble walking sometimes. So after the delivery, she'd felt lighter and was able to walk with no pain. The story about running up the stairs was true – she'd actually done it a couple of times just to prove how wonderful it felt to not be pregnant any longer.

Zahir listened, laughed and made all the appropriate sounds to Luca's stories and Callie couldn't help but remember how attentive he'd been five years ago. Until they'd come back to his country. But she couldn't blame him for that, she thought, trying to be fair. The man had been in the middle of a war, after all. And when he was with her they'd spent their time together in his bed, making love with each other and….Callie sighed, rubbing her forehead as she tried once again to figure out her life. Everything was falling apart!

She was glad that Zahir was giving Luca his undivided attention now. It was sweet the way the two were talking, catching up. Luca asked Zahir questions about everything from shaving to where he lived. They walked into the enormous kitchen and Luca easily found the container filled with the cookies he'd baked yesterday.

Callie sat on the other side of the counter, perched on a stool and wishing that…well, she wasn't sure what she was wishing for. She couldn't wish that Luca hadn't been born because he was the light of her life. If she hadn't met Zahir, where would she be? She definitely wouldn't have Luca's special presence in her life.

She sighed, catching the attention of both males and she looked up guiltily.

"She does that a lot," Luca whispered to Zahir.

Zahir nodded, leaning closer to his son. "What does it mean?" he asked.

Luca looked over at his mother, that devilish smile on his face. "I think it means she wants you to kiss her," he told her. "She hasn't been kissed in…" he paused, "well, never. Mommas and daddies should kiss. My friend Tommy told me his parents kiss a lot."

Callie's face immediately started burning and she shook her head. Okay, so she had been thinking about Zahir's kisses. And a whole lot more, but that didn't mean…

"Don't Zahir," she said when he started to walk around the counter.

"We have been ordered to kiss by the future Sheik of Larcatia," he commented. "I cannot ignore a command," he told her so that only she could hear.

She jumped off of the stool and backed away. "You're the sheik!" she told him. "You outrank the little devil," she argued.

He laughed softly and Callie also heard Luca's laughter as he climbed up onto the counter, happily eating cookies while he watched his parents "dance". "True. But perhaps I don't want to ignore the command."

She backed up again, heard her son's giggle and stepped around an overstuffed club chair. "Maybe I do!"

"Maybe you don't. Maybe you want me to kiss you."

She could see the message in his eyes. He was remembering all those times she said she was too embarrassed to try something he wanted to do to her but he wouldn't let her hide behind her puritan inhibitions. He would do it anyway and she'd always been amazed at how wonderful his ideas felt once she just released herself and let him have his wicked way.

She lifted her hands, trying to ward him off. "Zahir, this is silly. We don't need to..." she was stopped from arguing any further by the expedient method of his arm whipping out and capturing her. How he'd gotten around that darn chair so quickly, she had no idea. One moment, she was standing there making sure she wasn't within arm's reach, the next moment, she was in his arms.

"Don't!" she gasped but again her protests were ignored as his mouth came down to touch her lips. All of her breath came out in a sigh as he gently caressed her lips with his own. This wasn't a passionate kiss but the desire flared up regardless. She could tell that he was trying to keep the kiss under control for Luca's sake. Callie's fists gripped his shirt even while her eyes darted over to the countertop where Luca was perched, his hand covering his mouth as he excitedly watched his parents kiss for the first time in his life.

"That's funny," he said.

Thankfully, Zahir pulled back. "You think it is funny to watch your parents kiss?" he asked, trying to look stern.

Luca nodded his head, his chubby cheeks still grinning. "When are you going to be married?" he asked. "Tommy's parents are married."

Zahir held Callie close as he explained, "We already are married. I married your mother in a secret ceremony five years ago. It was so secret, no one even knows about it. Some of the people who work for me have released a press announcement providing the news of our marriage as well as your existence."

Callie's entire body tensed up with those words. "A press release?" she whispered through stiff lips. "Why would you do that?" Her worried eyes moved to Luca, her mind frantically trying to figure out how to keep him safe in light of this news coming out.

Zahir felt her stiffen next to him and knew what she was thinking. "It will be okay," he promised her softly. "First of all, no one knows that we are here.

Secondly, this house is built to protect the three of us. There are guards all around the perimeter and a state of the art security system. All of my men are well trained."

Callie couldn't really argue about this. Not in front of Luca. But as soon as her little man was tucked into bed, she was going to let loose on Zahir. How dare he do all of this without consulting her first? How dare he take her son's life and future into his own hands?

"Why don't we figure out what we're going to do about dinner, shall we?" she suggested, changing the subject.

"I'll have the housekeeper cook something up," Zahir said.

Callie whipped around, glaring at the man standing next to her son. "I'll make dinner, Zahir. I don't need a housekeeper to make meals for me." She glanced over at Luca. "Right, my man?"

Luca glanced up at his newfound father, his eyes serious as he said, "You don't want to argue with her, Dad." In a lower tone he said, "She might be dieting. She doesn't like to eat out when she's dieting."

That caused Zahir's eyes to come right back to Callie and they drifted down her figure, causing yet another one of those blushes that she hated so much. "Maybe we should show your mom that she doesn't need to diet. That she's perfect just the way she is."

Luca's shoulders went up and down in a mini shrug. "I tell her I think she's pretty. She just tells me she needs to lose weight."

Zahir shook his head. "We need to try harder."

They gave each other a conspiratorial look and Callie was shocked that, after only a couple of hours in each other's company, Zahir was already teaching her sweet little man his ways!

She stood there staring at the two of them, struck anew by all the similarities. They had the same eyes and hair, Luca was much taller than most of his peers which made sense since Zahir was about six feet three inches tall, much taller than the average male. And Luca's little arms were thin, but already showing signs of the muscles he would have. Just like his father's amazing physique.

"Why don't you show your dad how to play that crazy card game you taught me the other night?" she suggested. That would give her time to cook and think. And some space to think without Zahir constantly touching her, blowing her thoughts out of her mind with his kisses or those disturbing, feather-light touches.

Luca immediately jumped down off of the counter and looked back up at his dad, eager to show him some of his knowledge. "This way," he told him, taking his hand and leading him over to one of the tables. "We brought cards just in case the house didn't have them here."

Callie watched, her heart aching for her special time with her son now that Zahir was back in his life. Before this night, Luca had only played cards with her, they'd sometimes cooked dinner together, they'd make pancakes on Saturday morning together…so much of that was going to change now! And she didn't want it to change! She loved her life! Her life might be dull and ordinary. Okay, so sometimes she longed for a bit of excitement and she dreamed of Zahir way too often. But her life was safe! It was comfortable! What right did he have to step back into her life and mess it all up? Just because he was Luca's father….!

She turned to the refrigerator, unable to look at the two men and absorb all of the implications of Zahir's return. It was too disturbing so she just banished it from her mind for a while.

She pulled out ingredients for pasta, grilling up vegetables in garlic and olive oil, grating fresh cheese and boiling the whole-wheat pasta. Italian was one of her favorite foods and, even though she was still trying to lose those pounds, she decided that tonight, with Zahir's return, she needed comfort food loaded with cheese instead of a plate full of vegetables. She even sliced up the thick, crusty bread and added garlic butter to their dining experience for the night.

"Everything is ready," she called out to the boys. They both looked up, their focus entirely on their card game. She'd been listening to them while she cooked, Zahir's voice deep and masculine compared to Luca's more child-like tones. It would be music to her ears if she wasn't so terrified of what would happen after this week. Or even after dinner.

No, she refused to be afraid of tonight. There were six bedrooms in this house. She could find her own bedroom easily. She'd just use the one right next to Luca's room and Zahir could use the master bedroom. There was absolutely no chance that she was going to share a bedroom with him tonight.

Zahir and Luca came over to the table and, before she could do it herself, Zahir had lifted Luca up into the air, dropping him right down into the heavy dining room chair. Callie glared at him with jealousy because Luca might be only four years old but he was solid! She had trouble picking him up these days, sure that his shoes were actually filled with lead instead of simply rubber soles.

"So what do you guys usually do after dinner?" he asked.

"Momma reads to me," Luca said, reaching out and taking a slice of garlic bread. "Yum! You put cheese on this!" he said with relish and took a bite.

Callie ignored the garlic bread, feeling self-conscious suddenly in the too-small tee-shirt. Comfort food was one thing, but she didn't need to add the extra calories to her meal. She settled for the pasta and red sauce, even foregoing the grated cheese.

Zahir knew exactly what she was doing and, when the cheese came to him, he sprinkled a layer of the good stuff over his pasta, then reached over and did the same to hers.

She opened her mouth to protest, but he shook his head. "I'll prove to you that you have the most amazing figure," he promised her, adding a wink.

Callie blushed and shook her head, taking her fork and tasting the food. Oh goodness, it tasted good, she thought, closing her eyes with the pungent cheese.

He opened a bottle of red wine, pouring two glasses and Callie stared at the wine with longing.

"Try it," he coaxed when she just stared, refusing to touch the crystal glass.

She shook her head. "I shouldn't. I haven't had wine in..." She couldn't remember the last time she'd had wine. And then it occurred to her. It was the night before that horrible capture.

She lifted her glass, her fingers shaking but she forced herself to take a sip. It was good, she thought. But she set the glass back down, not wanting to remember how he'd taught her to enjoy wines. For three weeks, he'd introduced her to the amazing world of wines and decadence.

Setting her glass back down on the table, she forced herself to concentrate on eating. "Luca, why don't you tell your dad about your newest favorite book?" she suggested.

Luca then went on to regale Zahir with all of the stories he loved. Including Harry Potter and Percy Jackson...there were so many. Her son was a voracious reader and, if he couldn't read the book because of the complicated words, they would read the stories together, snuggled up on a rocking chair or in the big, soft club chair in her den area.

Those times were gone, she thought. Her appetite was gone and she pushed the food around on her plate, wishing that she could just turn back the clock.

Chapter 5

Zahir watched as Callie walked out of the bedroom, not looking any more refreshed despite the fact that he'd allowed her to sleep alone. She was fully dressed, but that was about it. His eyes roved over her long, sexy legs revealed by the shorts she'd chosen for the day. He liked them, he thought. He hadn't ever seen her in shorts. Five years ago, it had been fall so she'd worn mostly jeans or those stretchy, legging things. He liked those fine but the shorts...yep, they had to be his favorite. Her legs weren't skinny and bony as so many other women preferred. Nor were they fat either. Callie's legs were longer than her short stature would suggest, and smooth with muscles underneath the soft skin.

Luca's head bounced into his line of sight, disturbing his perusal of his wife. He'd been carrying his son on his shoulders as they talked together down on the dock, watching the mist dance across the surface of the glass-like lake. It was early in the morning and both of them had woken up and gone down to the water, just talking about stuff and learning more about each other. "Momma looks tired," Luca commented as if he too were worried about her lack of sleep.

Zahir looked at her delicate features and had to admit that she looked pretty exhausted. Those dark circles were getting worse, he thought.

"What's wrong?" Zahir asked, moving closer to her. He and Luca had been discussing the possibility of fishing again today but maybe they should do something different. He didn't want her to have the same reaction to worms that she'd had yesterday.

He lifted Luca off of his shoulders and put him into one of the dining chairs. The housekeeper that had been retained for the week had already cut up a fruit salad and there was an egg casserole in the oven, ready to serve. Luca and Zahir had only been waiting on Callie before they ate breakfast.

He held her chair out for her, winking at Luca's huge eyes as he watched his father treat his mother with manners that had never occurred to him before.

"Nothing is wrong," she said as she pulled the napkin from the table, spreading it out on her lap. "What did you make for breakfast?" she asked, smiling at Luca.

45

Luca shook his head as he used both hands to lift his milk glass carefully. "Dottie made breakfast. Did you sleep well last night?" he asked before taking a huge sip of his milk.

She rubbed her forehead. "I'm fine," she smiled.

Luca rolled his eyes. Turning to his dad, he said, "She didn't sleep well. She does this a lot."

Callie reached out and tousled his dark curls. "I'm fine," she promised.

Luca shook his head. "She's not fine."

Callie laughed slightly. "Oh, you think you know me so well, eh?"

He wiggled in his chair as Zahir set the egg casserole onto the table. "Why didn't you sleep well last night?" he asked as he took his chair opposite her.

Callie was exhausted, but there was no way she was going to admit anything to Zahir. Especially not with that knowing look in his eyes. "I slept perfectly fine."

Luca lifted his plate so that his mother could serve him the food. "She doesn't have that vibrating thing." He set his plate down carefully, unaware of the stunned silence above his head. "She always has trouble when she doesn't use that vibrating thing at night."

Callie's eyes went from her son's dark head to Zahir's amused gaze. "Do you need a vibrating thing to get to sleep at night?" he asked softly, trying very hard not to burst out laughing.

Callie shook her head, her mouth opening and closing in horror. "I don't...there's no..." she wasn't sure what to say. "I don't have a vibrating thing, Luca!" she finally announced with a strangled voice. Her hands were gripping the table as she looked around, terrified that someone other than Zahir had heard her son.

"Yes you do," Luca argued. "That thing beside your bed. It vibrates and helps you sleep. You said so yourself."

Callie's face was already red with total humiliation and she wasn't sure what to say.

Zahir's large, calloused hand was covering his mouth as he tried to smother his laughter. "Honey, you can just do away with your vibrating thing now. I'm here. And I'm more than willing to help you sleep at night. Just give me a chance."

Callie made a strange sound, her hand coming up to her forehead as she struggled to figure out what was happening to her. "Oscillating!" she practically screamed when she finally figured out what her son was talking about. "Luca, the word is oscillating!" She looked across the table at Zahir who was still trying to stop laughing. "I have an oscillating fan beside my bed! It keeps me cool at night and the white noise helps me sleep!"

Zahir couldn't stop laughing, so delighted with her embarrassment and her adorable blushes. Callie was so horrified by what their son had just implied and she looked like she'd prefer an earthquake to separate the ground beneath her so she could just fall right into it. "Ah, my love. An oscillating fan still won't be as good as what I can do for you. I guarantee that you will sleep better once you let me help you."

Callie covered her face with her hands, not sure how to get the horrible man to change the subject. "Stop it!" she mumbled. "Just stop going there."

"Oh, we're going there. In fact, I think that several new vibrating..." he couldn't finish that sentence because Callie was leaning over the table, her hand covering his mouth with her hand.

She could still see the laughter in his eyes but she glared at him with everything she had inside of her. "Don't you dare finish that sentence," she threatened.

Luca was looking back and forth at his parents, fascinated by this new turn of events. Callie looked at her son as she sat back down in her chair, then up at Zahir who was still chuckling. "What are you planning to do today?" she asked.

Zahir ran a hand over his mouth, trying valiantly to smother his amusement. "How about if we go sailing?" he suggested.

Callie thought that was a great idea, but she leaned over slightly, looking down at the dock through the large windows. "You don't have a sailboat," she pointed out.

"A minor technicality which will be remedied."

"Are you going to get a sailboat today?" Luca asked, almost standing up in his chair with excitement. Only his mother's stern glance kept him from genuinely breaking the rules.

"It is being delivered in," he glanced at his watch, "thirty minutes."

Callie tapped her fingers against the table, trying to find patience. "Zahir, we need to discuss this," she told him.

Zahir lifted a dark eyebrow in question. "What's to discuss? Do you not want to go sailing? I thought it was something you'd always wanted to do."

She was startled that he'd remembered that. It was just a passing comment she'd made one day. She couldn't even remember the context. "I do. I would love to go sailing but..."

He turned to Luca. "Finish your breakfast. Then go talk to Ms. Fisher. She'll get you ready for sailing."

Luca shoveled his food into his mouth, then jumped down from the table. He was already sprinting to his bedroom when he skidded to a halt, ran back to the table and picked up his plate and glass, carefully carrying them over to the sink. "Bye!" he saluted, then disappeared.

Callie was proud of him for remembering to clear his dishes but she turned to face Zahir. "You're spoiling him," she said, not holding back. "I don't want him to grow up into a spoiled, rotten kid who thinks he can have everything he wants."

Zahir leaned back in his chair, watching her carefully. "He's a good kid, Callie. What you need to understand is that he will have a great deal of responsibility on his shoulders. I will teach him to take his pleasures when and where he can."

She sat there, unable to move for a long moment as the reality of what was on her little boy's shoulders hit her fully. "And that includes buying a sailboat on a whim?"

He chuckled. "Actually, it wasn't a whim. Sailing teaches a person ways to listen to the world around them. A good sailor has to read the water and the wind, to use the earth's natural resources to move along the water. It is a powerful lesson. Using natural resources not only for energy but also understanding nature in humans, knowing that the people he will come into contact with during his lifetime will generally have their own agenda and he'll have to use that agenda to forge a better way for Larcatia."

Callie was astounded by his thinking and had no argument against such logic. She understood, but she didn't have to like it.

"Fine," she grumbled.

Zahir chuckled at her grumbling acceptance. Standing up, he grabbed her hand and pulled her out of her chair as well. "Sooner or later, Callie, you're going to trust me."

Her chin lifted up defiantly. "I trust you, Zahir."

Zahir looked at her pretty eyes that had changed to a light brown instead of their normal soft amber. He knew what he had to do with his son. But when it came to Callie, she was becoming a mystery. He knew that she still loved him, but she wouldn't let herself admit that and he didn't understand why. Or maybe he did and he just wasn't acknowledging how deep her fears went. It was a strain to keep his hands off of her, to listen to her signals and respect them. Last night had been one of the hardest nights of his life, keeping his hands off of her and letting her sleep alone in that bed down the hallway had been painful.

His hand lifted and gently stroked her golden hair. "How about if we just enjoy today? No worries about the future. No worries about anything, just relaxing and enjoying the sunshine and the open water."

Callie looked up into his eyes, trying to be reassured by his words. Unfortunately, she wasn't the kind of woman who could ignore the future. She done that once and Luca was the result.

"I would love to go sailing with you today. But that's all I can promise."

Zahir smiled and dropped his hand from her hair. "That's good enough for me. For today."

Luca had already changed his clothes and sprinted down the hallway towards them. "I'm ready!" The little man who stood barely four feet tall looked up at his parents with an enormous grin splitting his adorable face.

Callie was not immune to his enthusiasm. "Then let's go sailing!"

True to his word, Zahir was an expert sailor. The day was absolutely perfect with calm winds and a gentle sunshine that warmed them as they skimmed along the surface of the water. Zahir had even arranged for a picnic basket to be made up so they stayed out on the water, just lowering the sails, while they nibbled on gourmet sandwiches, handmade potato chips with some sort of delicious cheese topping on them, fruit and all sorts of decadent desserts.

The whole time that they sailed, Callie sat towards the back of the boat, content to watch her son and Zahir interact. She was amazed at how much knowledge Zahir had about sailing, impressed also with the patience he had with Luca who was excited to try everything, to touch everything, and wanted to do everything himself.

By the time Luca and Zahir maneuvered the sailboat back to their private cove, Callie was more than ready to put her feet onto dry land. The rocking of the boat had lulled her all afternoon. That plus the lack of sleep the previous night made it hard for her to keep her eyes open. She didn't want to miss anything, so she struggled to stay awake.

The dastardly and always observant Zahir noticed her fatigue and as they tied up the ship, he suggested that she go take a nap. Callie shook her head, knowing that if she took a nap at this point in the day, she would be up all night and wouldn't be able to sleep again. From experience, she knew that staying up and just pushing through the fatigue was her best option.

"I'll be fine," she said.

"Can we make cookies?" Luca asked.

Callie opened her mouth to tell him that she was too tired to make cookies this afternoon, but Zahir quickly nodded his head. "I'll make cookies with you, if you can show me how to do it."

Luca's dark eyes turned to Callie, silently begging for permission.

Callie chuckled at the idea of Luca trying to make cookies without her or Ms. Fisher. Luca was more into the tasting aspect of cooking making rather than the science or deliberation side of the event. But a devilish thought struck her at that moment. "Sure!" she replied, trying to hide her smile. "Your dad taught you to sail, it is only fair that you teach him something as well. So go for it! Make cookies. But remember that you'll have to clean up whatever mess you make."

Zahir looked down into her eyes carefully, understanding her expression but not sure what she might be hiding. "What's going on?" he demanded, taking her hand and pulling her closer. But Callie had anticipated his move and she slipped her hand out of his and backed up several steps on the dock, careful to not get too close to the edge. "Luca wants to make cookies with his new dad," she said, pretending innocence. "What could possibly go wrong?"

Luca grabbed Zahir's hand, pulling him up the pathway to the house. Zahir looked at her even as Luca tugged him up the path. "I'm going to regret this, aren't I?"

Callie laughed, all the exhaustion from the afternoon fading away as she eagerly shook her head. "It's going to be awesome! Just wait!"

Zahir shook his head, knowing that his little woman was up to something but he couldn't figure out what the problem might be. "There's no recipe?" he asked.

Callie waved her hand. "Oh, there are tons of recipes. If you don't find one in the kitchen, there are millions of recipes on the Internet that could help you out."

He didn't buy it. "We don't have all the ingredients?"

She chuckled. "Luca and I anticipated many afternoons making cookies. We have plenty of supplies for just about anything you might want to bake, not to mention all of the additional supplies that this house already has." She grinned as Luca continued to pull Zahir away. "Trust me," she tried very hard to have a sincere, innocent look on her face as she said "if there is any ingredient that you need that the house or my supplies don't have, I will be more than delighted to drive to the grocery store and pick up that additional item."

Zahir thought that he was adequately warned about this event simply by the look in her eyes. He just couldn't imagine how difficult it might be to bake cookies.

Three hours later, Zahir suddenly understood how evil his wife could be. Those kind, innocent eyes of hers had hidden depths of evilness that even he could not have imagined.

The kitchen was filled with smoke. Again! All of the smoke detectors in the house were now in a heap on the dining room table, there were no available cookie trays, and the cookie trays that had already been used would have to be trashed because of the burnt batter that was now permanently welded to the surface of each cookie sheet that they had stuck in the oven. Zahir had no idea what was on the floor of this kitchen, but no matter where he stepped, his shoes would crunch or stick.

"This was not as easy as I thought it would be," he said to his laughing son. The two males stared at each other, Zahir stunned by the amount of flour and batter and, he really hoped that was a pecan hanging from Lucas hair. Zahir suspected that he looked just as messy.

Grabbing his son around his waist, Zahir carried Luca with his hands and feet dangling in front of him as he went in search of his wife. He found her sitting on one of the comfortable deck chairs, looking beautiful and clean. She looked so serene as she stared out at the lake, the book that she had been trying to read was laying on her lap, face down.

He ignored the stunned expression on her face as he approached, still with Luca dangling from his arm. "Tell me the secret, woman!"

Callie stared, taking in the tall, formidable man in front of her. This could not be Zahir. It was simply impossible to think that the man who had confidently sailed around the lake, tilting that boat to a forty-five degree angle and pulling it right back up again, never capsizing the boat, sure of where all the rigging was supposed to go, how the boat was supposed to be sailed, how the winds could give them more speed or slow them down or turn them, could be trounced by cookie baking. She laughingly looked up at this man standing in front of her with her little boy, almost completely covered in flour and…what was that hanging from Luca's hair?

Callie tried very hard not to laugh at the sight in front of her but it was just too much to ask of anyone. She lifted her hand to cover her mouth but it was pointless. Laughter burst out of her, and she couldn't stop as she continued to survey the two males. Luca just grinned from ear to ear while Zahir tried to intimidate her with his Sheik–stare.

Luca turned around and looked up at his dad, and both males shrugged at each other, not exactly sure what was so funny. Unfortunately, that only made Callie laugh even harder. Zahir set Luca down onto the deck, and that was Callie's first clue that she was in serious trouble. Unfortunately, she didn't move quickly enough. By the time she realized that she was in trouble and had jumped up from her chair, Zahir was already too close. The arm that had previously been holding her son was now wrapped around her waist and she was being lifted into the air. Zahir spun her around so that she was now facing him, her hands manacled behind her back by one of his hands.

The laughter died out of her as she stared up at him with huge, wary eyes.

"Are you going to tell me the secret?" he demanded.

Callie couldn't stop the bubble of laughter that burst out of her. "If you're going to try and intimidate me," she said, "then you have to get the batter off of your face. The flour on your eyelashes doesn't do your 'bad-angry' stare much help either."

"Oh, you think I'm not intimidating?" He growled. "Let me see if I can become a bit more intimidating," and he leaned in and nibbled at her lower lip.

This was something Callie hadn't been expecting, but she should have. There was no way that Callie could say that she truly knew this man, but she knew his tactics. She knew the things that happened between them when they touched or when he took her into his arms.

So she should not have been surprised when he kissed her, or when his free hand slid up her waist. But she was. Nor could she stop the moan that escaped her lips at his touch.

The childlike giggle to their right caused Callie to freeze. Thankfully Zahir also lifted his head turning slightly to stare down at his son. "I think your next lesson is how to be a good wing man," Zahir explained to the giggling toddler.

Luca's curious gaze almost caused Callie to erupt into laughter again. Especially when his head tilted to the side and he said, "What is a wing man?" Obviously, he was more than ready to learn anything from his new father.

Zahir sighed but he pulled back again. "Don't think you're getting away with anything. We will continue this part of our discussion later." He dropped his hands from her wrists and waist then stepped back. Callie's eyes instantly dropped lower on his body, then shifted to see if Luca had noticed anything strange about his father. Thankfully, her son was too absorbed in a rabbit that had just hopped onto the property. But Zahir looked at her with a determined glare as he shifted slightly in his pants.

Callie suspected that a strategic retreat was in order. She stepped around Zahir and moved towards the stairs of the deck. "I don't understand why you think that making cookies is so difficult." She opened the sliding glass door and stepped into the great room of the house. But that was as far as she got. Her eyes took in the kitchen. Nothing else could enter her consciousness at this moment as she wondered if a hurricane had passed through the inside of this house over the past few hours.

There was flour everywhere, batter hanging from even the light fixtures on the ceiling. How in the world did they get batter on the ceiling? Luca was on one side of her and Zahir was on the other side and she looked at both of her men, then back at the kitchen then at both of them again. She still didn't get it. "What happened?"

Both Luca and Zahir shrugged their shoulders at the same time then looked back at the catastrophe of the kitchen. Luca took her hand and Callie tried not to shudder at the stickiness of his fingers.

Luca spoke up in their defense. "I think we did something wrong."

Callie stepped closer to the kitchen, her steps careful as she surveyed the damage to the once beautiful and elegant environment. "How did...?" She stopped. Callie decided that she didn't want to know.

She lifted her hands, relieved that she could drop the sticky fingers of her son, and said, "You go take a bath and get some clean clothes on. I'll start cleaning up."

Zahir was having none of that. "No way. All of us will go shower and change for dinner. We are going out."

Callie shook her head and started moving towards the kitchen. "This has to be cleaned up. It will be even worse if the batter dries and hardens on the..." Her eyes once again rose to look at the light fixtures. And the ceiling. And above the stove.

"You guys go get showered and when you're finished you can help me clean up."

Zahir shook his head. "You're not cleaning this up. I have a very capable staff who will clean this up. Go change and meet us out here in," he glanced at his watch, "thirty minutes." He looked up at her. "Will that give you enough time?"

She opened her mouth but he stopped her with a raised hand. "No, Callie, you are not cleaning this up. I am taking you out to dinner and by the time we return, this will all be cleaned up. No arguments."

Callie wasn't really comfortable with that mandate, but she figured she could start cleaning once he had gone into his own bedroom to shower.

Once again, he read her mind. "Callie, go in to get ready or I will pick you up and make sure you are in the shower," he warned. His voice had turned deep and husky and Callie knew exactly how he would ensure her compliance with his orders.

She didn't like it, but she also knew when to retreat when confronted with a difficult situation.

She almost stomped into her bedroom while Ms. Fisher took charge of Luca. When they were alone later tonight, she was going to have a stern discussion with him about him telling her what to do.

She was absolutely not going to bow down to all of the ways he wanted to change the raising of their child!

Chapter 6

"Goodnight, sweet little guy," Callie whispered to Luca who could barely keep his eyes open. It had been a good day, she thought. All things considered. Dinner out had been delicious with fresh catfish and hushpuppies, always a good choice but she suspected that the restaurants around Lake Anna were not the usual style that Zahir was used to. The man was a sheik after all. He ate in five star restaurants. The fried catfish was amazingly delicious, but it was from a diner where the service was friendly and warm-hearted versus deferential and intimidating. She and Luca loved it. And Zahir didn't seem to be disturbed by the family style ambiance, but she wasn't going to guess at what he was thinking any longer.

"Momma?" he called out when she'd reached the doorway.

"What's up, honey?" she asked, pausing to turn and look back at him.

"He's not going away again, is he?" Luca asked sleepily, snuggling against his teddy bear.

Callie wished she didn't know who he was talking about. "No. He'll be here in the morning, my man," she assured him. She suppressed the tears that sprung up to her eyes, wishing that he didn't want a dad as much as she knew he did. She wished that she could be enough for him, but that wasn't the case. Luca had met and already fallen in love with his father, and that was as it should be.

"Will he take me swimming tomorrow?" he asked.

Callie laughed softly. "I'm sure he will if you ask him tomorrow."

Luca grinned from the pillow. "I already know how to swim. You taught me so I won't be a problem to him. I promise."

Callie's heart broke as she realized that her little boy thought his father had gone away because he was a problem. She hurried back to his bedside and knelt down. "Oh Luca, you're never a problem. You're the best thing that happened to me."

His little fingers played with the ears on his teddy bear, obviously nervous and confused about his father's sudden presence in his life. "But he didn't want to be with me. I just now got big enough."

She shook her head again. "No, honey. That's not why he wasn't with us. I told you that he's a very important person and his main priority was keeping us safe. He couldn't be near us and do that. You believe me, don't you?"

He considered that for a long moment, but in the end, he was just too tired to make sense of this new development in his young life. Callie leaned forward, kissing him again on his chubby cheek. "We'll talk about it more in the morning. And maybe your dad would like some of our special pancakes. What do you think?" she suggested.

Luca smiled but rubbed his face against the soft fur of his teddy bear as the sleep took over.

She pulled the door almost all the way closed, wanting to be able to hear him if he woke up during the night. She then made her way to her own room. Well, the room she'd decided to use for the week. She'd had to search out her clothes yesterday because the uber efficient and never seen staff had stored them in the master bedroom. They all thought she was just going to fall into bed with Zahir and…she shivered at the very idea of that action. It was impossible, she told herself. As she had several times since his reappearance, she pushed the idea out of her mind, not letting it take root. She had to be strong! She had to find the willpower, otherwise…she'd be mush.

She wanted to discuss Luca's words with Zahir, to let him know that his son was worried about what might happen in the future. But she was too scared of what might happen now that they were alone, and not in the distant future but right here, right now. She could almost feel Zahir's presence even though she couldn't see him. It was almost as if she could sense his thoughts and knew that he wanted to make love to her tonight.

She absolutely could not let that happen. She was overwhelmed by his presence and everything that it implied not to mention Luca's instant love for the man. No doubt about it, she was in a complicated mess and she had no idea what to do, except continue to be as strong as possible.

So she took the coward's way out and went into the bedroom. She washed her face and brushed her teeth, feeling very proud of herself for not giving in to the pull of need that was ever-present when Zahir was close by.

She pulled on her nightshirt and, for one moment, she wished that she had something sexier, more sophisticated than the drab nightshirt. It was completely unflattering but soft and comfortable. Which is pretty much the way most of her wardrobe was. She went for comfort more than sophistication.

But no matter how soft or how comfortable, she couldn't relax in the enormous bed. She was too painfully conscious of the fact that Zahir was here, in the house, probably waiting for her to come downstairs again. He'd let her sleep alone last night, but she suspected that tonight would not be the same.

Sure enough, ten minutes later, the door to her bedroom opened up and she held her breath, trying to pretend to be asleep.

"It isn't going to work, Callie," Zahir growled as he walked over to the bed.

Her eyes popped open and, for a split second, she thought about scooting over to the other side of the bed. But that pause was her downfall. He was there, scooping her up into his arms and carrying her out of the bedroom.

"I don't want to sleep with you, Zahir," she told him.

"Good. I hadn't planned to do much sleeping anyway," he told her as he carried her down the hallway and into the master suite.

That made her breath catch in her throat and she couldn't believe what he was implying. Or maybe she could, but she didn't want to acknowledge it. "We can't have sex either."

He laughed softly as his foot kicked the door to the master bedroom shut. "I don't remember any problems the last time we tried it, my dear."

Callie shook her head, her mind shifting into overdrive as his words hit her. She started to struggle, but he just let her legs drop down while, at the same time, his mouth covered hers.

And just that easily, he overcame all of her objections. Callie tried to fight the desire. She was proud of herself for all of maybe five seconds while the heels of her hands pushed against his chest. But then he shifted his hands, cupping her full breasts that were pressing against that darned nightshirt and she was lost. Worse than lost, she was ravenous for his touch.

Suddenly, instead of trying to push him away, she was pulling him closer, her body needing him in a basic, elemental way that flashed through her mind, creating a furnace fire of heat within her that could be put out only one way.

When his mouth moved to her neck, she leaned back, her hands pushing against his shirt, needing desperately to touch his skin, to feel all of him once more. All of the memories of this man, of the way he would touch her, make love to her, came rushing back to her mind, filling her with the most delicious anticipation. Gone were all of her resolutions to stay away from him, to not let this happen. Five years of wanting erupted as he continued to touch her and she was almost crying with her need to feel him inside of her.

His teeth nibbled then his lips soothed, but there was no soothing the nuclear passion that was inside of both of them. They'd been apart for five, long years.

Zahir felt her shivering and couldn't slow down. This was his wife, the mother of his child and no other woman had ever compared to her. From the first moment he'd seen her, she had been the one that had driven him mad with desire. He ripped her underwear off, discarding it so that his fingers could delve into her wet heat. "Callie!" he roared.

She lifted her legs, wrapping them around his waist and pulling him closer, needing all of him. And when he slipped inside of her, she gasped as her body stretched, her back arched and her eyes practically rolled back into her head. "More," she pleaded, her hands fisting in his hair as if he might move away from her.

"Yes," he growled back and he moved deeper into her heat, filling her up then waiting for her body to adjust to his size. He had to remind himself that she was a tiny woman. He had to take this slow. She felt so tight, so hot and he shook his head, trying to regain just a small bit of control so he didn't tear her apart.

But his perfect Callie was having none of that. Her hips lifted, inviting him to move, demanding that he move. And so he slid out of her, watching her mouth open as the sensations made her crazy.

This was what he loved, what he'd been craving for years without her. Because of all the years apart, it took only a few strokes before Callie was splintering apart into an explosive orgasm. And with her tight sheath squeezing him, Zahir couldn't hold out much longer either.

He held her close, his body trying to protect her but it was just too good, too amazing to be in her arms, to be holding her once again.

When the vibrations slowed enough, he rolled over, pulling her with him so that she was draped across his chest, still intimately connected to him. He let his fingers glide down her back, over her adorable, round bottom and then back up again while he listened for her breathing to come back under control.

Callie realized what was happening, what had just happened and was shocked. Pulling away, she tried to get up off of the bed, to move away from him but he was having none of that. And since her body was still thrumming with pleasure, she didn't have the energy to fight him just yet. She'd give herself a few minutes, then head back to the other bedroom. There was no way she could...

"Please don't..." she whispered and shifted so that he was no longer filling her. Moving off of him, she tried to get her mind back in order. But then his hand moved around to her stomach and he pulled her back against his chest. Her body was once again on fire for him. She might have just had the best climax of her life but this was Zahir. She was more than ready for round two but she didn't want to give in. She had to be strong at some point, shouldn't she?

"Don't do what?" he asked, sweeping her blond hair off of her neck and kissing the sensitive skin on her nape. "Don't do this?" he asked, nibbling on her ear. She shivered, closing her eyes. "Or do you want me to stop this?" he asked, as his fingers trailed down her naked spine, finding all of those erogenous zones that he'd discovered during their three week relationship so long ago.

When she arched her back, her bottom pressed against his erection and his hands moved lower, pulling her thigh back so that his own could slip between her legs. His hands pulled her sleepshirt over her head, tossing it onto the floor behind them. That gave him better access to her breasts and he used that access perfectly, his hands cupping her breasts, his fingers tweaking her nipples.

Callie was once again lost in the sensuous spell that he could so easily weave over her body. "Zahir," she whispered, shifting her leg higher against his and pressing her chest into his hands. His mouth and teeth continued to tease her back and shoulders while his hands drove her crazy with his hands and fingers. So when he slipped into her wet heat again, she was completely on board, even pushing against him to deepen the movement. And just that easily, they were moving in that rhythm that took her higher and higher. It wasn't as fast in coming this time around, but mostly because Zahir was controlling their pace, not letting her move against him as fast. So when she exploded, the pleasure was so intense she had to grab his hands, begging him to stop the pleasure on her breasts. It was too much and she couldn't take it after so many years. His hands moved down to her hips, holding on as he pressed into her harder and faster. And suddenly, she was climbing that cliff once more, arching her back as yet another orgasm swept over her just as he found his own fulfillment.

Afterwards, she collapsed against the mattress, her body so sated, she couldn't even move. Nor could she push Zahir away when he pulled her against his chest. The last thought she had was the realization that she still had no willpower where this man was concerned.

Chapter 7

Callie watched as Luca and Zahir played in the water. She hadn't stepped into the lake since arriving, preferring to cool off with the shower that had been installed on the deck instead. Every time she tried to jump into the water, her irrational fears about bugs and dirt crept up and she shook her head, stepping back to her deck chair, picking up her book and letting the boys continue playing.

It was now the end of the week and she wasn't sure what was going to happen. Luca had blossomed under Zahir's presence. Before, he might throw a temper tantrum when he was too tired or too hungry. But the two times it had happened this week, Zahir had calmly pulled him aside and explained that he was not allowed to do this. He was a prince and others would look to him for how to behave. If he started to throw a fit, then others would think it was okay. And it isn't okay.

The first time Callie had heard Zahir try to explain that to Luca, she thought about intervening. Luca was a four-year-old boy. He was hungry and tired, it was normal for him to express himself since he didn't have the words. But as she watched, her amazing son pulled himself together, nodded to his father and walked as calmly as possible back to Callie. The feeling was still in his eyes and her heart contracted with love for the little man who was trying so hard to impress his father. She'd gotten him some food or helped him settle down for his nap. But it had only happened twice and she wasn't sure she liked that. She wanted him to be a little boy.

When she'd argued with Zahir about that, he'd disagreed. "He isn't just a little boy," he'd explained with absolute finality. "He will be a ruler someday, Callie. He has to start learning this at an early age."

Callie didn't agree, but she also knew that there wasn't much she could do about it while Zahir was around.

But that begged the next question, what was going to happen when Zahir left? Luca loved him! Luca worshiped Zahir! What was going to happen when he was gone?

She didn't want to think about that, so she pushed the issue out of her mind, glancing down at her book. She would discuss that tonight after dinner, when Luca was in bed and he couldn't overhear their conversation.

She gritted her teeth, thinking about what normally happened after dinner. Zahir waited in the hallway for her after she tucked Luca into bed. And there was no way of denying him. He simply didn't wait long enough for her to tell him no. As soon as the lights to Luca's room were turned off, Zahir swept Callie into his arms and made love to her for the rest of the night.

Callie was quiet during dinner that night. They were scheduled to leave tomorrow and she had no idea what was going on inside his head. She wanted to talk to him about that, but conversations of that magnitude would take courage. And she also needed time alone to figure out what was going on inside her mind. She didn't have either.

She was afraid to talk to Zahir about their plans because that would mean facing a future with or without him. Which one did she want? Which would be healthier for herself and Luca? She had no idea. Nor did she know which outcome she even wanted. No matter how hard she tried to avoid Zahir's arms, she still fell into them every night, enjoyed the passion and sensuality that Zahir could give her. And lately, she hadn't been trying very hard to avoid his arms and his bed.

As she watched her boys talk, Zahir telling Luca stories about his country and the people, she wondered what it would be like to go back with him. Was it really different? She'd grown up with stories of countries that had been fighting with each other for decades. Those countries negotiated peace then started fighting again. They claimed to want peace, but they were too busy fighting to really try for peace. And his country had been fighting with its enemies for years! How could they move on and want peace? How could Zahir guarantee that war wouldn't break out again?

But, in this case, it wasn't as if a whole generation had been raised to know war. A decade was a long time, but it was only ten years. People remembered the peace before the war. Could it work?

Or was she just setting herself up for a crushing disappointment? And what would happen if they went back to Larcatia and war broke out? Callie had been watching Zahir teach Luca how to be a leader. It was amazing to see her little man try to imitate his father, but he was still a little boy. Would Zahir want his son by his side if war broke out again? Would Zahir teach their son how to battle? Would he be in the line of fire? Would bullets be racing by her son's head?

The thought of Luca in a war zone chilled her body despite the August heat.

She looked up, suddenly realizing that there was silence.

"What's wrong?" Zahir asked.

Callie's skin was cold as worry over the future washed over her yet again. "Nothing," she replied, forcing herself to smile.

Zahir wasn't fooled. She was worried about something and he was tired of her trying to hide her concerns from him. How could he show her that things would be okay if she didn't talk to him? "You're not eating your dinner."

Luca straightened up. "You promised you wouldn't try to diet this week, Momma," he admonished her.

Callie had to laugh because only six days in Zahir's presence and he was already taking on his father's commanding tone and his mannerisms. "I'm not," she assured him.

His eyes looked down at her plate, then at his own and his fathers, while her dinner had barely been touched. "Then why haven't you eaten any of your dinner?"

Callie glanced down at her plate, realizing that Luca was right. She'd barely touched the grilled chicken and salad she'd made for dinner. Looking over at Zahir's plate, the two pieces of chicken and enormous salad she'd served him were gone and more than half of Luca's was finished. She was the only one who hadn't been able to eat anything. "I guess I'm just not hungry tonight," she told both of them. That was the truth, but she knew that there was so much more to it than just appetite.

When she took the plates away, she avoided Zahir's too-knowing eyes as she stacked the dishes into the dishwasher.

She felt Zahir touch her shoulder and she spun around, gripping the countertop behind her.

"Sorry," he said and the concern in those dark eyes soothed her faster than his words could. "I'll get Luca ready for bed. You look tired."

She smiled, grateful for his help. "Thanks," she said and pushed her hair back off of her face. Zahir moved closer, pressing her body gently against his. "What's wrong?" he asked softly, his hand smoothing the hair she'd just pushed out of her way. "You've been tense all day long."

She forced a smile, but it wasn't very convincing. "You've been keeping me up most nights," she replied. "I'm just a bit wiped out."

His fingers continued to smooth back her hair and he didn't look convinced that a lack of sleep was her biggest concern. "We'll just sleep tonight," he promised her.

Callie's lips compressed uneasily. "Sleep?" she asked, feeling her chest tighten with his promise. This was their last night together. Why was he going to let her sleep? Did he not want her any longer? Had she done something last night to turn him off?

"Stop," he commanded with a gentle but firm tone.

"What?" she asked, more than a little breathless, both from her thoughts and fears as well as the way he was touching her.

"Something is going through your mind and it most likely isn't good."

She laughed a bit because he was right. "Like I said, I'm just tired."

"You're on vacation. Why don't you let the household staff do the cleaning for you?"

"We've discussed this, Zahir. I don't like being surrounded by servants."

Zahir sighed as he pulled her closer, not sure how to help this stubbornly independent woman. Resting his chin on her head, he searched his mind for some way to get her to accept her position in his life. She was his queen, although he'd never really told her that much. She should have deduced it by now though. But looking around, he knew that this wasn't his normal world. He'd instructed his guards to keep to the woods as much as possible and he'd dismissed his other staff, wanting this time with Callie and Luca to get to know them once more. The guards and servants were on standby and knew to appear quickly when needed and disappear when they weren't.

Other than her refusal to be pampered, he was thrilled with the way the week had gone. His son was a boy a father could be proud of. He was smart, adorable, considerate and observant. He was everything his people would need to lead them.

Callie was still the kindest, sweetest woman he'd ever met. And their passion had only increased over the week as he'd reintroduced her to the sensuality of her body. She'd suppressed it over the past five years, but it hadn't taken him long to get her to accept this aspect of her personality. He still initiated all of their lovemaking, but she was a very active participant. The only downside to the week was that she hadn't admitted her feelings for him. He wanted to hear that she loved him but she was holding back, still refusing to accept that they would be together. And since she didn't believe they had a future, she wouldn't admit her feelings.

Chapter 8

"It is time, Callie," he told her the following morning as he held her close.

Callie tensed, wondering what he meant. She thought about that statement, knew that she needed to ask the question but there were two questions she could ask. And she didn't like the answer to either of those questions.

She closed her eyes, wishing she could stop this moment from happening. "I don't want this week to end."

He kissed her again. "I have to return to Larcatia."

She didn't want that to happen. Either she wouldn't see him again or he wanted to bring her with him. Both bad scenarios. "No," she whispered, denying both options.

His hands slid up and down her bare arms, feeling the goose bumps rise up. "I've loved our time here together. But we must return."

She heard that "we" and didn't like that at all. But she couldn't deny that there was a surge of relief in knowing that he hadn't planned on leaving her. She thought about that for a long moment, but then shook her head. "I can't go back, Zahir. I just can't do it."

He took her hands and led her over to one of the sofas. "I have to return. This was our honeymoon, the time together that we were denied after our wedding."

She tried to pull her hands away but he only held them more firmly in his. "The wedding I didn't even know that we had," she told him with a grimace, still angry with him for that little omission.

He wasn't going to tell her that their marriage was already being celebrated by his entire country, not to mention in Tularia, Altair and Lurasa. All four countries regarded his marriage as more evidence that things were going well. "Yes, well, I have a great many responsibilities. And I need you by my side. I need my son to be introduced to his people. And I need you, Callie. I need you to be with me and help me."

Five years ago, she'd wanted that so badly. She'd been thrilled when he'd taken her to his homeland and had dreamed about hearing those words. She'd loved Larcatia and all of the warm-hearted people she'd met. Until that one man. Those three days, three nightmarish days and nights of hell in one man's sick, demented world. She shook her head. "I can't do it," she said and the trembling started up again. She buried her face in his chest. "I just can't go back there. I went with you the first time and I was so in love with you that I didn't care that there were scary things that I should be afraid of. But now I know and…" her voice cracked at the idea of what she'd gone through.

Zahir hadn't wanted to tell her this, but if it would reassure her, she had to know. "He's dead, love," he told her.

Callie's whole body froze. "What do you mean?"

"He's dead. The man who kidnapped you, he's gone. He will never hurt you again."

She looked up into his dark eyes, her soft, golden ones unsure about what he was saying. "What do you mean? And how can you be sure?" She felt her heart pounding in her chest and her skin turned clammy.

He kept his hands on her waist. "I am sure."

She shivered, thinking that he wasn't going to come right out and tell her, but she suspected that he'd killed that horrible man.

Callie knew that she should be relieved. But it bothered her that Zahir's soul was now marred by that gruesome man as well as hers. "You didn't have to do that," she whispered fervently.

Zahir couldn't believe she was saying that. Any man who hurt his family knew the consequences. "He hurt you. I could not let him get away with that. But you don't need to worry about him. Never again can he hurt you."

She shivered. "I still can't go back there, Zahir. Why can't we just leave things the way they are?"

He sighed and let his hands drift through her golden hair. "Because things always change. And I will not leave my wife here. I would never ask you to be without Luca either."

She gasped as the pain of not seeing her son stabbed through her heart. "You'd take Luca?" she asked, but she could see the answer in his eyes.

"I will not take him away from you. But yes, he must come home. He must learn to rule his people."

She didn't like the sound of that. "He shouldn't have to do this," she told him, falling back on her anger. "He should be allowed to choose his future."

Zahir took her hand and led her to the cars that had been waiting patiently. "Luca has a future. He will decide how to rule Larcatia."

Callie felt defeated but she had to rally. This was too important. For all three of them. She had to fight for their future and somehow, they had to all be together. "There has to be an alternative," she begged, not getting into the limousine.

Zahir had to be firm. "There is no alternative, Callie. You are my wife. I want you by my side and Luca needs you. We are returning to Larcatia today." He wanted to be patient with her, but he couldn't give her more time.

"I won't go!" she told him, panic welling up inside of her. She tried to be brave, to fight for both herself and for Luca, but looking into his eyes, she knew that it was a pointless effort. As the truth of their future settled into her mind, anger and tears welled up. She couldn't be without Luca and Luca was going back with Zahir. Rationally, she knew that this was what needed to happen. It was the right thing to do. But she shook her head, angry at how fate had twisted her comfortable, safe world so suddenly.

"I won't love you, Zahir! I will hate you for making me do this."

He kissed her forehead, ignoring the way she tried to pull away. "Then I will have to find ways to make you happy."

Zahir continued to stand there, looking down at her.

Callie considered running away, but she knew that she wouldn't be able to get far. Nor would Zahir let her run. He was too close and his reactions were heightened by years of war. He was a soldier and she could see the determination in his eyes.

In the end, she got into the car but only because she was determined to protect her son. And she had faith that she would eventually figure out a way to convince Zahir that living in Larcatia wasn't the best solution for any of them. She had to be smarter, more creative in her arguments. This was a battle she could not lose!

Chapter 9

"We should have to pack up the house," she said, watching sadly as the guards put the last of the suitcases into the trunk.

Zahir shook his head and laughed slightly. "That will be the first thing you're going to have to get used to, Callie. Servants will pack up and close down the house."

Her lips compressed with that news. "I don't think they'll..."

"They'll close it up correctly. And we'll come back. I promise."

He took her hands and tried to comfort her. Luca was close by, playing basketball with one of the bodyguards. "That's his personal guard, isn't it?" she asked, looking at the way the man watched Luca so carefully.

"Yes. His name is Junar Alfirsi. He'll defend Luca with his life if that becomes necessary. Junar will also teach him many things, like self-defense and combat training. As will I. There will be numerous classes that he will enjoy."

"And a whole bunch he won't like, right?" she shifted in the car, resentful already. She wanted to teach him to make pancakes and cookies, decorate Christmas cookies and how to dance and treat a lady. Zahir wanted to teach him to kill, to maim and to combat one's enemies.

As Junar led Luca over to the limousine, she scooted as far away from Zahir as possible, focusing all of her attention on strapping her son into his car seat. She knew she wasn't being fair, but nothing about this situation was fair, in her mind. She ignored the fact that Zahir had taught Luca to sail and fish, to explore the woods, seeing things in different ways. Weren't those all survival techniques? Weren't those still combat related?

She sighed, rubbing her forehead as she worked out everything in her mind. This was not the way she'd always pictured her marriage and her life to go. She didn't need the palace or the servants. She didn't even care about the limitless clothes budget. All she wanted was to love her son and her husband, to spend evenings listening to what had happened during their day and fight over which bills to pay or argue about which Christmas party to attend.

The flight to Larcatia was uneventful but Callie ignored Zahir. She was so hurt and angry right now. Or perhaps it was just her fear welling up to overwhelm her. She wasn't sure and she couldn't really think rationally right now. No matter how much she wanted to resist, she knew, deep down inside, she acknowledged that Luca needed to discover Larcatia. Not only was he the future ruler, it was his birthright and she had no right to deny him that.

When they landed, she'd already changed into an ice blue suit, one that looked great with her hair. She had no idea when Zahir had ordered her a new wardrobe, nor did she care. Besides, he probably hadn't ordered it but had simply asked someone on his staff to order appropriate clothes. Although she would admit that it was nice to wear something elegant. It boosted her confidence as she faced the uncertain future.

When she stepped out of the airplane's bedroom, Luca's eyes widened. "I like that one much more than your others, Momma," he said.

She looked down at her suit, feeling pretty and feminine. But her other work suits weren't too bad either. Okay, so this one seemed to fit her perfectly and the material was better than anything she'd ever worn before. "What's wrong with my other suits?" she asked, ruffling his curly hair.

"They don't make you look pretty." He stood up and took her hand. "This one makes you look beautiful." And he looked over at his father, obviously seeking approval.

Callie caught the look and her throat constricted. Zahir was already teaching him things, such as how to treat a woman. It suddenly occurred to her that those were things that she could tell Luca, but until a man told him, a man that he respected, then he wouldn't really follow the guidance.

It was yet another example of how much Luca needed his father and her heart wrenched that she'd denied her son this example for so long.

The flight attendant stepped out of the galley area. "The captain says that we're about to land."

Callie made sure that Luca's seat belt was strapped in place before she found a seat as well. Luca's face was plastered against the window, his eager, curious mind wanting to see as much as possible from the air.

She thought about looking as well, but she couldn't do it. Instead, she placed her hands in her lap, refusing to let them start wringing again which would reveal her anxiety. She wasn't nervous, she told herself firmly. She was strong and confident and she was going to figure out a way out of this mess!

The plane landed with barely a bump and then taxied over to the special gate set up specifically for Zahir's takeoffs and landings. The security in this airport was heightened with not just the ruler coming back home, but also the crown prince in the form of an eager four year old, clutching the ear of his teddy bear as he took it all in.

Callie stepped off of the beautiful plane in front of Luca and Zahir but he put a hand to the small of her back, guiding her to the line of vehicles. She knew that she was stepping out carefully, almost resisting each step, but she couldn't help it. She finally ducked into the back of a black SUV, shivering as she realized that this vehicle was bullet and bomb proofed. Just the need for that kind of defense made her stomach queasy.

She watched as the convoy approached the palace and her heart thudded with dread. Would it be that bad again? Could something happen to Luca? Or to Zahir? She didn't want to be kidnapped and dumped into a dirt prison again, but the idea of either Zahir or Luca enduring what she'd gone through made her almost sick. She didn't want to think about it, but the closer they got, the more anxious she was.

She hadn't been taken from the palace, she reminded herself. She'd been shopping in the market, looking at the various goods on display. She breathed deeply, carefully trying to control her anxiety.

The SUVs pulled up into the main gate of the palace and she was stunned by the pageantry that was on display. The palace guards were in full dress uniform and even the household staff was standing outside, their smiles huge as they waited to greet their returning ruler and their future prince.

"They know," she whispered.

Zahir knew what she wasn't asking. "It was announced as soon as the treaty was officially signed."

"How long ago?"

"Three weeks. I arranged to come get you as soon as it was final but preparations for our week together started long before then." He took her hand once more. "You see, Callie? It really is going to be okay."

She turned her head away, not wanting to face this reality.

He stepped out first, then held a hand to assist her. She took it, but pulled away as soon as she was out of the vehicle. Luca and Ms. Fisher stepped out of the SUV as well and there was an enormous cheer as the palace staff got their first glimpse of their future ruler.

Zahir bent down and lifted Luca into his arms, handing the teddy bear to Ms. Fisher. Callie had to laugh at that and was relieved that Luca didn't need it at this moment for reassurance. She would make sure that the bear found its way into his bedroom though. There was no way she would allow Zahir to take that security blanket away from Luca until her little boy was ready for that to happen. There were just some things a little guy needed, and a teddy bear was one of them.

She followed Zahir and Luca, pretending that she wasn't swelling up with pride at the two men in her life. Zahir carried Luca over to the staff and formally introduced him to his advisors and council members. Each of them bowed in front of Luca who turned to his father, not sure what to do.

Callie watched with astonishment as Zahir briefly acknowledged each person, then chuckled when Luca wiggled out of his father's arms. Standing straight and with more dignity than she'd thought possible in such a young man, Luca mimicked his father's acknowledgement of the bow by each person. In that moment, Luca captured their hearts and loyalty and Callie's eyes stung with tears she refused to shed.

With each small lesson from his father, Callie was discovering that her need to get away was growing less and less intense.

Chapter 10

Callie watched Luca sleep for a long time. Her heart ached for him and for all of the burdens that were eventually going to be on his little shoulders, but she also knew that Zahir was going to help him get there.

What was she going to do? The idea of staying here filled her with an almost choking sense of doom. She felt safe here in the palace but was she supposed to stay here for the rest of her life?

She didn't want to live like that, but the longer they stayed, the more she realized that she couldn't separate Zahir and Luca. Those two were like peas in a pod.

Oh, and there was also the realization that Zahir hadn't been using any form of birth control. How could that little detail have slipped her mind over the past week? They had made love so many times, she would be shocked if she weren't already pregnant.

Goodness, the possibility filled her with both excitement and dread. She would love to have another child with Zahir, but doing so would eliminate any possibility of her leaving him and going back to Virginia.

Or was that possibility already gone?

She smoothed down Luca's hair, smiling at the way he was clutching his teddy bear so tightly. He didn't seem to be upset by his future, but there was no way he could grasp what was coming. He was just too little and his world, mentally, revolved around the here and now.

So how was she to keep the little guy, who loved cookies and ice cream, while Zahir started teaching him how to handle a sword?

"Come to bed, Callie," Zahir said.

She turned her head, not able to see him in the darkened room. "I'm fine," she told him. It felt like she'd given in on so much lately so, right now, she was going to sit by her son and watch him sleep for as long as she wanted.

"He's asleep, Callie. Come to bed."

She shook her head, just being stubborn now. She didn't even look in his direction this time. "No. I'm not coming to bed with you. You've bulldozed me enough for one day, Zahir. Just leave me alone."

Zahir sighed and, because Callie wasn't watching him, she didn't see the hurt look that entered his dark eyes that was quickly smothered. Zahir looked at his woman's tense shoulders and shimmering eyes in the dim light of his son's bedroom and wished there was something he could do or say that would make her feel more comfortable about all the changes that he was imposing on her previously simple life. But his mind was blank. He knew that, in the long term, she would be better off and he could make her happy. But right now, she was hurt, angry, resentful and overwhelmed by everything. "Okay, come to bed when you're ready. Just don't wait too long. It has been a long day and you're exhausted."

With that, he walked out of Luca's bedroom, leaving her to her tortured thoughts.

In the end, she really was exhausted so she moved back to the bedroom where one of the servants had told her all of her clothes had been moved. This room was different from the one that she'd shared with Zahir before. Or maybe it was the same one? Just different decorating? She wasn't sure. This room was softer, more feminine. Zahir's suite had been filled with leather and dark colors. This suite was decorated in yellows and blues. She liked it, but she wasn't sure why Zahir would...

Yes she did. She sighed as she realized that this was another attempt from him to make her feel more comfortable. Her heart ached at the gesture and she once again fought the falling feeling she experienced every time Zahir did something kind or generous for her. It was all part of his master plan to get her to fall in love with him again.

What he didn't realize was that she was already in love with him. Good grief, she'd never fallen out of love with him. She'd just pushed all that pain in her heart aside and learned to live. Day by day, breath by breath. And now she was set up to be hurt all over again.

She walked into the dressing room and surveyed her nightgown options. There were about a dozen silk nightgowns in one of the many drawers and she sighed, her fingers touching the delicate material. The lace and silk were meant to seduce. She had to laugh because, if she stepped out of the dressing room in one of these nightgowns, it would be on the floor faster than it took to hear the slithering of the material down her body.

Zahir was a passionate man and giving him the temptation of her body in one of these would only increase his desire.

Perhaps that's what was intended. Perhaps it was all a mad conspiracy by the palace staff to get more little princes and princesses. She wouldn't doubt it.

Or maybe Zahir was the one to have directed these little slips of nothings. He wanted a large family. They'd talked about having several children five years ago. But they needed to talk about that again. She wasn't sure what she wanted anymore.

What was she talking about? One moment, she was determined to get away, to figure out a compromise that didn't include her living here. And the next moment, she was wondering how many children Zahir wanted?

Was she crazy?

Perhaps she was, she thought with a sigh. She stood up and walked into Zahir's closet. Pulling down one of his shirts, she carried it into the bathroom and got ready for bed. She had no idea where he was, but it would be really nice if he didn't come back to the bedroom before she fell asleep.

Callie took a long shower, reveling in the multiple showerheads that surrounded her with warm water. With the press of a button, the showerheads switched to steam while she used the scented soap, shampoo and conditioner.

After a long time under the warm spray, she finally accepted that it was time to get out and try to get some sleep. She suspected that tomorrow would be just as stressful as today. She needed to get some sleep so she could be ready for whatever Zahir threw her way.

She dried off and pulled on the white shirt, rolling up the sleeves so that her arms could come out.

When she stepped out of the bathroom, she came to a halt. Standing right in front of her was Zahir, his shirt off and the top button of his slacks undone.

His dark eyes traveled up and down her figure, obviously appreciating the sight. "The staff forgot to provide appropriate sleepwear for you?" he asked, amusement lighting his eyes.

Callie gripped the neckline self-consciously. "There are several silk gowns in one of the drawers."

He chuckled as he moved closer. "You ignored them, knowing that they wouldn't be on your delectable body long enough for me to fully appreciate them, is that it?"

She grimaced. "Something like that," she replied. No, exactly like that, she thought silently. And tinging that comment was a large dose of resentment at how easy things seemed to be for him.

"I'm not going to fall in love with you," she lied. Her revelations from earlier were haunting her, making her feel more vulnerable than she ever wanted to feel. And she still couldn't alleviate that panicked, choking feeling that kept welling up inside of her every time she thought of…that pit, the nights, the bugs.

"I can't…"

He was there in a flash. Zahir had seen her eyes change color, her skin pale and her whole body tensed. "Shhh…" he pulled her into his arms. "I'm here. He's gone." Zahir wished the monster was still alive so he could kill him again for what he'd done to this gentle woman. He pictured what their life could have been like if it hadn't been for that man. If not for the sick bastard, Zahir never would have been separated from his Callie, he would have been there for his son's birth, for his first steps, the first time Luca smiled or laughed or spoke. He gently held Callie in his arms, willing her to absorb some of his strength.

He hated that she was so scared. He knew that she loved him but couldn't admit it and he wanted to break the man who had done this to her.

"Let's go to bed," he told her and lifted her up into his arms. He didn't make love to her that night. But nor did he sleep. He just laid in the bed with Callie in his arms, listening to her breathing. He suspected that she didn't sleep either and he wasn't sure if he blamed her. After what she'd gone through, he closed his eyes, trying to block it from his imagination. He knew all too well what one human being could do to another.

Chapter 11

The following morning, Callie woke up and she was alone in the bed. Still dressed but the larger shirt was more revealing than what she was used to. She tugged the shirt closed over her breasts, wondering what had happened. All she remembered was that terrified feeling coming over her and then Zahir holding her in his arms. She realized something else as well – she hadn't been having those nightmares since Zahir returned.

It was a nice feeling, she thought. But then she pushed it away and stepped into the shower. She had to figure out what her future was and it definitely wasn't this, she told herself.

She needed to figure out options, to discover the possibilities. And she couldn't do it while lying in bed.

Suddenly, Zahir burst into the bedroom. "Wear something pretty," he told her.

She looked up at him, draped only in a towel. "Excuse me?" she asked, clutching the towel above her breasts.

He walked into her dressing room and selected a pretty, yellow suit with a flowered scarf that would drape becomingly around her neck. "Will you wear this one?"

She looked at the beautiful suit he was holding in his hands by the hangar and couldn't stifle the laughter. "If that's what you want."

"Oh, you know what I want, but we're on a mission today."

She shook her head as he handed the suit to her. "Fine. But are you going to tell me what this mission is?" she asked.

"No. Luca is starting lessons today which leaves you in my care. Get dressed."

Callie could see that he wasn't going to tell her anything. "Fine. I'll wear this. But you have to leave while I get dressed." She watched him, hugging the suit close to her and waiting to see what he would do. Would he leave or was he going to stay and do something naughty?

Callie could honestly say she wasn't sure which one she wanted more.

When he walked out of the room, winking at her as he left, she breathed a sigh of relief. She dressed carefully, putting on light makeup and tying her hair back into a conservative knot. Since he wouldn't tell her what they were doing, she wasn't sure what she should prepare for. But it was certainly nice that she didn't have to worry about what to wear. If Zahir thought the yellow suit was a good choice, she was relieved to have the decision taken out of her hands.

Unfortunately, she should have been more assertive when questioning where they were going. As soon as the armored SUV stopped, she knew what he was going to do. He lifted her carefully out of the vehicle and steadied her when she looked around. "I don't want to do this, Zahir," she said, her eyes huge as she took in the busy outdoor market. "Please don't do this to me."

Part of Zahir wanted to let her get back into the SUV and hide in the palace but he knew that she had to do this. Until she knew that the world was safe, relatively safe, then she would still be constricted by her fears.

"Just take a few steps for me, okay, love?" He wrapped an arm around her waist, trying to help her in any way he could think that might work. "Let's just walk over to that basket," he said, indicating a large, woven basket on the edge of the market. "After that, we'll come back to the car."

Callie knew what he was trying to do and a part of her knew that he was right. But that was the rational part of her brain. The irrational side of her was screaming to run and hide, that there was evil here.

But he was right. And if she could just step over to the basket, she'd be fine. It wasn't like there were any other people in this area. She looked around, noticed guards all around her. They weren't watching her, they were looking at the others in the marketplace and they were searching the shadows, the faces of the people milling about. In other words, they were fully aware of what she was going through and they were all trying to help her get through this.

She straightened her shoulders at that point. He was right. This was exactly what she needed. She might hate him for making her face this fear, but he was right. Damn him, she was going to do this and get it over with.

She pushed away from him, refusing his help and she wouldn't allow him to force her. She would show him that this was fine and then she'd demand…well, she wasn't sure what she would demand of him. Right now, all of her focus was on that basket, on the people milling around just outside of this perimeter.

"Face your fears," she whispered to herself. With each step, she chanted those three words to herself. Over and over again, she said it until it was a rhythm in her brain. She reached the baskets and looked around. Her heart was pounding, she felt as if her whole body was drenched in sweat and she wanted to run screaming from this place. But then she realized that she was fine. No one had attacked her. No one had swept her up into his arms, thrown a hood over her face and stuffed her into a trunk.

She was fine.

Callie took several deep breaths. Farther, she thought. "I'm going to do this." She stepped into the people, looked over at the guards. They were all completely aware of what she was doing and moved with her. Step by step, she walked deeper into the market. The last time she'd been here, she'd lost track of her guards. She'd been so interested in what was for sale, smelling all of the different spices and feeling the various fabrics. She suddenly realized how wrong she'd been to have lost track of her guards. It hadn't occurred to her before now how much of her capture had been her fault. She'd blamed Zahir, the guards, the man... but she knew now that she'd lost her guards. And they'd lost her. Yes, they should have kept better track of her. That was their job. And Zahir should have listened to the intelligence chatter that day that had warned him that there was an imminent threat.

But she'd never once acknowledged her side of that day, her fault and what she could have done differently. She'd been so angry. And with that realization came a power she'd never considered before now. She looked over at one of the guards. He glanced at her, then around at the other people milling about, then back at her. One by one, she observed the guards as she stood there. Each of them were diligently scanning the crowds and then coming back to watch her.

The monster hadn't captured her to hurt her personally, although he'd done an excellent job of that. He'd captured her to hurt Zahir. She'd been a political target, not a personal one.

And in fact, she was still a political target, but now it was dawning on her how much responsibility that put on her own shoulders.

She turned around and looked at Zahir through new eyes. He had a great deal of responsibility on his shoulders as well.

How did all of this make her feel? She wasn't really sure, she thought.

She nodded to her guards, then walked over to Zahir. "Let's go," she said softly.

Zahir was so proud of her, he wanted to lift her into his arms and hug her, to carry her off somewhere and make love to her. But he kept his hands to himself. She'd looked strange a moment ago and he wasn't sure what that look meant and until he understood more about what was going on inside of her head, he had to hold back, give her space.

Hell, he wasn't sure if *she* even knew what she was thinking right about now.

When they returned to the palace, she quickly stepped out of the vehicle and, before he could ask her where she was going, she was almost running down the hallway.

"Keep an eye on her," he commanded to the team of guards who had been selected to protect her.

Three of the guards broke away, one of them speaking into his radio.

Zahir rubbed the back of his neck. He had a council meeting, briefings from several of his advisors, numerous contracts to review and more work than he even wanted to contemplate. So instead of walking down the hallway to find his wife, he turned to the right and walked into his office. Callie needed time alone, he suspected. And he thought she might be furious with him. But that couldn't be helped.

She loved him and he damn well wanted her to admit it to him!

He pushed himself to work hard for the rest of the day, focus on the issues. Callie needed her space and no matter how much he wanted to go to her and hold her, he had to respect that she needed time alone.

Or maybe she didn't.

Hell, he didn't know anymore. Maybe he'd pushed her too hard this morning. Maybe she was a basket case now and he'd have to put her into a straightjacket. They'd had three weeks together five years ago and one week now. He needed more time to really understand her. What he couldn't do was to let her go. Maybe, if Luca hadn't been born, he might have been a better man, he might have been able to sacrifice his own happiness so that Callie could stay away from Larcatia. If his son didn't need his mother and if Callie…

He couldn't let her go. There was just too much at stake. He was tired of wanting her and only her. He needed to make this work! She needed to know that he would do anything in his power, except let her go.

When the last of his meetings adjourned, he stood up and walked out of the administration area of the palace. He had to find her, he thought. He'd been getting updates on Luca all day long and knew he was making huge strides. But the guards watching Callie had informed him that she'd been sitting by the west garden all day long. She hadn't eaten, she hadn't really moved.

He was worried.

Ignoring anyone who tried to stop him to ask a question, he barreled through the hallways, intent only on finding Callie to make sure she was okay.

When he finally reached the entrance to the gardens, he looked across the pathways but he wasn't reassured. She looked so still, so sad. Her golden hair was no longer held back but now cascaded over her shoulder and the scarf she'd knotted around her neck lay on the stone bench beside her. Even her shoes were off.

But it was the stillness in her that worried him the most.

He approached her as if she were a wounded animal, cautiously, slowly. Making sure that she knew he was there so that he wouldn't startle her.

Callie looked over at him and his heart wrenched at the sadness he saw there in those beautiful, amber depths.

"I've always hated this time of the day," she said softly. Looking up at the sky, she blinked at the setting sun. "It always feels like I should be more productive, as if

I should be doing something but the hour before sunset is depressing to me. It's as if the day is winding down and I haven't done enough."

The muscles in his throat constricted at the idea that she needed to do more than face those debilitating fears earlier this morning. "You've accomplished a great deal today."

Callie turned her attention away from the pink and gold rays of the setting sun so she could look up at her husband. Huh! She played around with that word in her mind, tossing it about and wondering about that part of her relationship, her life. Husband. She'd acknowledged that she was married, after a long argument with herself and him, but the word 'husband' had never really struck her in regards to Zahir. "What's your favorite time of the day?" she asked.

"Anytime I'm with you or Luca," he quickly replied.

Callie smiled and some of the sadness eased from her eyes. Her fingers were still, he realized. He wasn't sure exactly what that meant because every other part of her body seemed tense. Normally, he could look at her hands, her fingers, to gauge how stressed she was but she was sending mixed signals now.

"You always know the right thing to do and say. Were you born with that talent?" she asked, glancing away again. "Or was it part of your princely training?"

Zahir wasn't sure how to answer her. "I've had a great deal of diplomatic training, if that's what you are asking."

She shook her head. "Not exactly the same thing." Sighing, she stood up. "Let's go find Luca and hear what he's been doing today," she said. And with that, she walked out of the garden, leaving Zahir still no clearer on what was going through her mind.

Chapter 12

"Pull on a pair of jeans," Zahir said, entering their bedroom the following day.

She glanced at him, startled by his command. "Jeans? I didn't think jeans were a good choice as your wife." She'd slept better last night than she had in a long time and she wasn't sure if it was because she'd dared herself to step into the market and face her fears, or if she'd finally accepted some things about herself and her life. Both, probably. She just wished she could figure out what she was going to do about Zahir. Goodness, she loved him and hated him. Those two dichotomous feelings were hard to reconcile inside her head. And she still felt like she was being backed into a corner, resentful of how he'd manipulated her life and complex fears, hopes and other confusing questions about her life, her son and her husband.

So it was no wonder that she wanted to both kiss him and kick him as he stood in front of her now telling her what to wear for a second day in a row. Yesterday it had been a relief. Today...well...she wasn't sure. Kissing and kicking at the same time came to mind.

He winked at her with a slow, devious smile. "Jeans are perfectly acceptable at times."

She liked this teasing, more flirtatious man more than the one yesterday who had been so stern and concerned. His casual attitude helped her to accept that today wouldn't be a bad day. "Like today?"

He nodded. "Or whenever I want to feast my eyes on your delectable bottom," he pointed out.

She rolled her eyes. "Jeans it is. They are my favorite thing to wear anyway."

He sat down on the chair and watched while she walked into the dressing room and sifted through her clothes. She wasn't sure where her jeans had been stored so it took her several minutes to find them in a drawer. When she pulled them out and turned, she realized that he'd been just sitting there.

"Have you been watching me the whole time?" she asked.

"Yes. It's been...enjoyable," he replied, letting his eyes skim down her figure, still just wrapped in a robe.

She glared at him, wishing that she knew what was going on in his mind. "You're being rude again, aren't you?"

"You love me. You don't mind if I watch."

The smile fell from her features and she clutched her jeans closer as if they could somehow protect her from his statement. "No, Zahir. I'm here because Luca needs a mother."

He shook his head. He wasn't going to let her get away with that excuse any longer. Not after last night. They still hadn't had sex since landing in Larcatia but he knew. She'd been scared two nights ago and she'd slept in his arms. And last night, she'd started sleeping on the far side of the bed, but quickly moved over to him, unconsciously moving her body as close as she could get to him. "No, Callie. You're here because you love me."

She started to get angry. And several other emotions that she didn't want to investigate too clearly. "Zahir, this is not about you and me. This is about what's best for Luca."

His eyes narrowed and he stood up from the chair, towering over her as if daring her to deny her feelings. He was getting angry now. "Are you really trying to tell me that you don't love me?"

She looked up at him, wishing that she could say the words, but her whole body started trembling at the idea.

He noticed her reaction and pulled back, but he wouldn't release her hands. Her inability to deny her feelings for him reaffirmed his belief. "You love me Callie. You wouldn't have given yourself to me at the lake house without that emotion to back up your actions."

She turned back to the closet, irritated with his confidence. "That's just sex, Zahir."

She stepped into the dressing room and closed the door, dressing by herself and away from his heated gaze. But even after she finished, she still stayed in the closed area, not wanting to go out there and face Zahir again. Yes, she was in love with him but that was for her and her heart to know. Admitting it to Zahir would eliminate the last barrier between them.

It hurt too much to be vulnerable.

She opened the closet door and found Zahir pacing back and forth in the bedroom. "I'm ready," she said, a part of her wishing she could ease his mind and tell him that she loved him.

She shivered when his eyes skimmed down over her figure in the figure hugging jeans. But still she remained quiet about her feelings. "Are you going to tell me where we're going?"

Zahir considered his plan for a long moment. If he followed through with his idea, he wasn't sure what her reaction would be. Would she be too scared to see the rest?

And dammit, she did love him! She couldn't touch him, be with him, give herself so completely to him every night and not be in love with him. Not his Calliendra! She simply didn't give herself away that easily!

And then it hit him. She was scared! She was afraid of what they felt five years ago and what it would mean for their future, not to mention how others could use it against her, Luca or even him again.

When he figured that out, and he hoped he was on target, he realized that his plan for the day was a good one. He could show her the places she needed to see and maybe he could convince her to release her fears, or, at a minimum, talk to him about those fears so they could work through them together.

Patience, he reminded himself. He had to have patience. "Yes. Let's go," he said and took her hand, pulling her out of the bedroom.

He led her to the helipad on the roof of the palace. But that was yet another obstacle. He'd had no idea that she was afraid of helicopter flight but he appreciated the way she clung to his arms, wanting to hold onto him. It pressed her breasts up against his bicep.

It took him several moments to convince her that the helicopter was safe, and that the pilot was extremely capable. "Would you feel better if I flew?"

Callie's hands fell on his chest, grabbing his shirt in her fists. "No! You can't get onto that thing either."

Zahir laughed. "Callie, do you have any idea how many hours I've spent in the pilot seat of one of those things?"

Her eyes widened and she clenched her jaw tightly. "Don't tell me things like that," she said, looking away.

He chuckled again. "My love, you're going to have to admit that you love me or not be concerned for my safety."

She sniffed slightly. "I'm not concerned for your safety. I just don't want anything to happen to you." When she saw his eyes light with amusement, she turned her head away. "There's a difference," she argued and unclenched her fists from his shirt.

He wasn't buying any of it! Every word out of her mouth, every gesture she made, told him that she loved him. She just didn't want to love him. "Yes, my dear. Come along. You're going to like flying in these. It is very different from a plane."

She didn't want to get onto the helicopter, but she wanted to go wherever it was that he wanted to show her. She was caught and the easiest route was to get on that silly contraption. "You're sure it is safe?" she asked again.

Zahir hugged her. "You're adorable when you're worried, my love. Come," he said and pulled her along.

As soon as they were strapped in, he plunked a headset over her ears and gave the signal to the pilot to go ahead. The rotors started swirling and the wind around them picked up. Moments later, they were flying through the air and Callie grabbed Zahir's hand, squeezing it hard. He turned his hand over and gave her his full attention, speaking into the microphone.

"Look to your left," he told her.

When she looked out the side window, she was able to see the entire capital city laid out beneath them. The city worked its way up the mountain with the larger houses perched nearer to the top. There was a river running down the side of the mountain that she'd never seen before. He explained that the river was fed from an underground source and the people never touched the water, believing that it was sacred. The water disappeared into a well in the middle of the city, eventually emptying out from a waterfall and going into the ocean.

As they flew, Zahir pointed out the various monuments of the city, the statues of the heroes from the previous war to the ones that had ended centuries ago. He explained the ancient buildings, how the architecture had evolved over the years and even the newest architect who was building the capital library, funded now that the war was over.

"The flight is over," he told her as the helicopter gently landed at the base of the mountain. "We drive from here."

She stepped out of the helicopter, relieved to finally be on the ground once more but she had to admit, at least to herself, that the ride had been interesting. And once he'd started talking to her, explaining the city and interesting points, she'd forgotten about her fears of the unusual mode of transportation.

"Come along. There's food in the vehicle already."

He drove out of the city, heading higher into the mountains. There were fewer and fewer vehicles around them now and she wondered how he'd gotten away from his bodyguards for the day.

The terrain changed almost suddenly. First there was just desert and rocks but when they came around to the other side of the mountain, she was surprised by all the trees and green plants. "What's this?"

"This side of the mountain gets all of the rain. The height of the mountains pushes the moisture higher, making the rain heavier and it falls. But as the air rushes over the mountain, all of the moisture comes out over here and the other side is too dry. So there's desert for the next hundred miles or so before it runs to the ocean."

"It's beautiful," she told him, amazed that such an oasis could exist in what she'd thought was a desert country.

"Wait until you see where we're going," he said and expertly maneuvered the powerful SUV around a bend in the road and came to a stop.

Right in front of them was a huge waterfall surrounded by grey rocks and lush vegetation. It was quiet, with birds chirping and a few animals rustling in the trees, but there were no other humans here.

"Where is everyone?" she asked, looking around and walking closer to the blue pool of water. Looking down, she could see that there was a deep cove, the rocks keeping the water clear. It turned murky on the other side as the water rushed over the dirt and the trees dropped things into the water, but right here, it looked like a pool.

"There are a few other people that venture here during the weekends, but during the week, it is pretty isolated. This is a hard area to get to. Most people walk the trail which should only be traversed by the more experienced hikers. So it isn't a huge tourist site. Too hard to reach."

"I love it," she breathed, sitting on one of the rocks and dipping her hand into the water. Her eyes widened as she discovered the temperature, which wasn't hot, but it wasn't cool as she had expected. "It's warmer than I thought it would be." She smiled up at him, surprised.

He chuckled at her expression. "The water comes from rain, not melted snow like it would in some places. So it isn't as cold as most people expect." He watched her dip her fingers back into the water, glad that she was enjoying this excursion better than yesterday's.

She laughed, delighted with his explanation. "I've never really visited any of the waterfalls in the United States so I wouldn't know how cold they are. I guess it is just my perception that the water should be cold."

He pulled a basket out of the back of the truck and easily hefted it over to the rock where she was sitting. "Hungry?" he asked.

"Starving, actually," she said and eagerly looked into the basket. "I spent too much time with Luca this morning instead of grabbing something to eat." She peered into the basket. "What did you bring?" And then she laughed. "As if you would know," she teased. Zahir didn't venture into the palace kitchens. He ordered someone else to cook whatever he might be in the mood for. And she didn't mind that one bit after the debacle of trying to make cookies at the house in Lake Anna.

"Yum! Chocolate!" she said when she started pulling things out of the basket. "Oh, and this looks interesting." She lifted a container filled with some sort of flatbread, rolled up and stuffed. "These look like pinwheels," she eyed the contents carefully. "There are all sorts of fillings."

"I wasn't sure what kinds of foods you like. We didn't spend a great deal of time eating, the last time we were together."

Callie blushed, remembering what activities they did spend time doing. And he was right, it didn't involve eating. The only reason they stopped for food was to re-energize so they could make love with each other again.

His eyes darkened as the memories flowed around them, almost like a silken caress. "You remember that, don't you Callie," he said softly. "The way we couldn't get enough of each other. The headaches we had because we woke up in each other's arms late in the morning, long after we usually would have had our coffee."

"Stop it," she whispered, taking out a container filled with strawberries. "It doesn't matter now. We're different people now."

"We're the same. The world continued to rotate, and we're still the same people, just with a bit more baggage."

She started to shake her head, but he ignored that. "We're older and wiser, but fundamentally, we're the same."

He paused to watch her for several moments, trying to read her body language. "What are you afraid of, Callie?"

"You're trying to convince me that I'm still in love with you but I'm not." She was holding the container against her stomach, trying to protect herself from his words. "I'm not. And I never will be. I won't be vulnerable ever again."

His hand reached out, his thumb rubbing her jawline. "Isn't it too late already?"

She put the strawberries down and peered into the basket. "Wine," she said, pulling it out with triumph. She found a bottle opener as well, even crystal glasses. "Too bad you can't have any of this," she said, desperately trying to change the subject.

"Why not?" he asked, accepting her change of subject. He would get her to admit that she loved him by the end of the day. He just had to follow his plan.

"Because you have to drive us back. No drinking and driving," she told him sternly. "Especially through those roads that can't even qualify as roads, if you ask my opinion."

He acknowledged her comment with a shrug of one of those massive shoulders and Callie's mind instantly snapped back to holding onto those muscular arms while he made love to her. She missed that, Callie realized suddenly. Goodness, it had only been two nights without him and already she was aching to be held by those wonderful arms again.

She jerked back to the present when he asked, "What do you like most about your job?"

Callie was relieved to have that subject to discuss, and get her mind off of making love with him. That was a taboo subject, she told herself firmly. They talked about business while she set out the food and she learned much more about the financial side of Larcatia. She was astonished to hear that Zahir was not just promoting oil, but he'd also spent a great deal of money on education from preschool to the universities, trying to lure people to the country to teach and learn.

"Is the investment paying off?" she asked.

"Yes. Many people are finding that this is a beautiful country and want to stay and live. They get their education here, then stay for the job. They are then able to teach and grow the economy."

She'd just finished what she thought was a lemon brownie but it probably had a different name here. It was delicious and she handed him one as well. "You're quite brilliant," she said, a light in her eyes that she wasn't even aware she was showing him.

"And you're quite beautiful," he told her. "And smart too. You've created some very good websites over the years. I like the ones for Erinson. They were hard, weren't they?"

Callie laughed but nodded her head. "Yes. When Marcia assigned them to me initially, I was excited. The requirements were a huge challenge. But even worse than the new technology I had to learn, they were a difficult client. Always wanting to communicate via e-mail, sometimes not responding for days even when a deadline was drawing near..." she looked over at him and a though occurred to her.

"The apartment building I live in, you owned that. And Ms. Fisher was your employee." She hesitated to ask this question but she had to know. "Were you Erinson?" she asked.

He nodded his head slowly, not sure how she would feel about that.

She put the glass of wine down carefully, thoughts flitting through her mind. "Why?" Even Callie wasn't sure how to feel about this latest revelation. She'd spent hours trying to satisfy that client, only to have them come back later and demand more.

He knew what she was asking and wanted to be honest with her. "Because it was my only communication with you. I needed some link, some way to be with you and so I had you build websites for my companies."

Her fingers shook as she fiddled with her napkin. "Will you come clean about the job?" she asked.

He sighed and leaned his head back, staring up at the sky. "Yes, Callie. The job was just a ruse. But only initially. You were hired on to work at the company, but no one, especially not Marcia or myself, thought you wanted to handle the technical work. Remember, you were just a receptionist at first. I thought it would be the perfect job for you so that you could enjoy your pregnancy and not be afraid any longer. I was trying to give you time to recuperate in the only way I knew how since you wouldn't go see a therapist and talk things out with a professional. It was your curiosity that had you designing websites the first day on the job instead of simply answering phones and greeting clients."

She nodded her head. "So that's why the job paid so much," she thought out loud. "You were a very busy boy." She looked at the trees and the waterfall. "Was any of it real?"

He sat up and looked at her again. "If you're asking if the job was real, yes. Eventually, you created the whole company. I never intended for you to have to work, but Marcia convinced me that you were good at the work and you liked it. You thrived in that environment, Callie."

She looked down at her hands. "Except that now I'm finding that it was just another part of my life that wasn't real."

He was getting frustrated now. And impatient with her continuous rejection of what he could provide for her. "What did you expect me to do, Callie? You were my wife! You were pregnant and I couldn't keep you safe and close. So I did the next best thing. I protected you in the only way I knew how." He watched her features carefully. "I didn't lie or cheat. I provided for you. I understood that you wanted nothing to do with me or my country and you were severely traumatized. But that didn't negate what we felt for each other. What I feel for you even now."

Her amber eyes flashed up to his. "What do you feel for me now?"

He sighed impatiently, running a hand through his hair. "I love you Callie. I have loved you from the moment I saw you and I will always love you. And the memory that you were hurt is killing me. Every time I think of you, in that man's hands, I go just a little crazy, Callie."

She shivered, recalling the time herself. "It was bad," she told him and wrapped her arms around her legs.

He pulled her onto his lap, holding her close. "Will you tell me about it?"

"No," she replied instantly, but she savored his touch, needing it more than she wanted to admit to herself.

Zahir sighed, kissing the top of her head. "You've never spoken to anyone about it, Callie. It's all locked up inside of you."

She turned her head and glared at him. "Have you ever been tortured?" she asked.

"Yes," he replied.

That stunned her and she wasn't sure what to say at first. But then she pulled her hands from around herself and hugged him. "I didn't know," she said, her voice cracking with the horror of what he must have gone through. "When?"

"It was a long time ago. During the early years of the war."

"And?" she prompted.

He sighed and shook his head. "I don't want you to hear something like that."

She lifted her head. "Zahir, why are you asking me to tell you about what happened to me, but you won't share your experiences?"

"Because you don't need to hear about them. But you need to release the fear that has been inside of you for too long."

She shook her head. "It's in the past." And with that, she stood up and started gathering the picnic items. "We need to get back. Luca will be finished with his lessons soon."

Zahir suppressed the automatic burst of frustration, striving for patience. "You will eventually talk to me, Callie. It is the only way we can move forward."

"Not true. We're moving forward now. We're gathering things up and heading back to our son."

"This is stagnation. When you admit that you love me, we can then move forward and be happy."

Callie held onto the blanket with all of her strength. She didn't like him talking like that. It frightened her and made the steel band around her heart tighten.

"I've told you numerous times, Zahir. I will not love you. I won't be that vulnerable again."

He took the blanket out of her hands and looked down at her. "You're afraid of being vulnerable but you already are, Callie. You're my wife and I will protect you. But you need to trust me."

She shook her head. "I trust you. I just won't love you."

They drove back to the helicopter landing site in silence, Callie unwilling to budge and Zahir not sure how to convince her to talk to him. When the helicopter landed at the palace, she moved hurriedly towards the schoolroom, eager to see Luca and find out what he'd learned during the day.

Callie ignored Zahir, wanting to put more space between the two of them. Her mind wondered what it would be like to talk to him about that experience so long ago, but she wasn't really sure if it would do any good. She still didn't want to be a target for his enemies. Loving him meant that she would become that target.

Luca came rushing out of the schoolroom as soon as she stepped through the doors. His eyes were bright and excited, eager to tell her everything that he had learned throughout the day. "Momma, did you know that dinosaurs used their scales and fins to keep cool? And a chameleon's tongue can be as long as his body!" Callie had to laugh when Lucas stuck his tongue out, his eyes going cross-eyed as he tried to look at the length of his own tongue.

"No, I had no idea that the chameleon's tongue was as long as his body. And actually I'm sort of glad that I never knew that. It is a bit of a frightening idea that any tongue can be that long."

Zahir's deep voice came from behind her and Callie was surprised that she hadn't felt him there before that moment but Luca continued to tell her about all the amazing facts he'd learned during the day. "Did you know that a male oyster can change to become a female oyster? And then, if he decides that he doesn't like being a male or a female he can change the other way again."

Zahir plucked Luca up lifting him into his arms. "What else did you learn today?"

Luca then proceeded to give his father an enormous list of factoids that he'd learned, his enthusiasm for knowledge evident. As Callie walked silently besides the two of them, she couldn't help but be amazed at the wide diversity of subjects that his new teacher had brought up with her little boy. Once again, Callie realized how good it was that Zahir had come back into their lives. Luca was an extremely intelligent boy and he needed the extra stimulus that one-on-one learning could give him. She was also concerned about how he was going to get his social time in, but she released that. At least for the moment.

Callie watched her son with Zahir, her eyes and her heart confused. Her brain was telling her that she needed to give in and release the past. But how was she to do that? How could she protect herself, her son, and Zahir when bad people still inhabited the world? Perhaps Zahir was right about talking. But she would never talk to him about what had happened to her. She just didn't want him to know. She had to protect him from her experience.

She looked down at her hands while she examined that thought in her mind. Silently, she considered the implications of her need to protect this man. And how exactly was she to protect him? He was so big and strong and he didn't have any weaknesses.

The muscles in her stomach clenched and the nausea rose up as her thoughts evolved into something that she didn't want to acknowledge in herself. She didn't want to love Zahir but she couldn't seem to stop. And it didn't seem fair that she felt this way. She'd told him from the moment she saw him again that she was not going to love him.

She suddenly realized that there was silence in the room. There were no more questions coming from Zahir and no more answers from her son. When she looked up, she realized that both of the men in her life were staring right back at her.

"What's wrong? Why aren't you telling us more about what you learned today?"

Luca looked at his father, obviously not sure what to say or do. When he looked back at Callie, his eyes were worried. "Momma, why are you crying?"

Zahir put Luca down, ruffling his dark hair as he'd seen Callie do on numerous occasions. "Why don't you go see if there are any cookies in the kitchen? I will try to figure out why your mother is so sad."

Luca tilted his head way back, trying to see his father. "You told me that I needed to care when a woman is hurt. And Momma is a special woman, so I should be extra concerned. And I don't like it when she cries. She used to cry in her sleep a lot but now that you're here with us, she doesn't do that anymore."

Callie hadn't realized that she was crying. Her hands lifted to her cheeks, and sure enough there were tears on her cheeks.

"Yes, you're right that you should be concerned. But I think that this is something between me and your Momma. Go find the cookies. But only have two because I don't want you to spoil your dinner."

Luca rolled his eyes. "Momma always thinks that cookies will spoil my appetite. But I think that boys need cookies in order to grow bigger. And I want to be just as big as you, Papa."

Zahir chuckled. "I don't think that you will have much of a choice about your height, son. Height is determined by genetics and all of the men in our family have been rather tall. And I don't think that cookies, or a lack of them, will affect your height significantly."

Luca looked exactly like his father as he considered those words and tried to form a pro cookie argument. "Is there any scientific proof of that?" he said, repeating a line he'd heard from his father.

Zahir chuckled. "There's my word for it. And you're going to lose your two cookies if you try to argue for more."

Luca understood that. His face was stunned for all of two seconds. And then his little body raced away, heading towards the palace kitchens. Callie watched him until he was out of sight, Junar right behind him.

When they were relatively alone once more, he turned to face Callie, his hands fisted on his hips as if he were bracing for the next challenge. "Okay, talk to me. What's going on?"

Callie sighed and wiped her cheeks once more. "Honestly, I'm not completely sure myself, Zahir." And she plopped herself down on one of the brocade chairs. "I'm very confused. On the one hand, I know that Luca is thriving here, with you, and he's needed you in his life for so long and I didn't even know it until you arrived."

Zahir sat down next to her. "And you? Do you need me in your life?"

Callie stared up at the ceiling, trying to stifle the tears. "I don't want to need you, Zahir."

"Because that too, will make you vulnerable." He didn't ask. He was understanding the words that she couldn't utter out loud.

"Yes," she nodded. "You make me feel things that anger and excite and drive me crazy and the whole gamut of other emotions. And I'm so confused and terrified of what will happen tomorrow or next year and it isn't fair that you can do this to me so completely!" She sniffed and wiped her cheeks again. "You're a bully and tender at the same time. Do you have any idea what that does to me?"

"Drives you crazy?" he suggested, trying to think of the words she'd just used.

"Yes! You drive me crazy! You swoop into my life, turn everything upside down. Not once, but twice! Five years ago, I was in college and having a fine time! Then you come into my life and show me all the things I hadn't known I was missing. I hadn't even believed most of them were possible!"

His dark head tilted at an angle as he listened. "And this is a bad thing?"

Her fury increased exponentially with that question. "Yes! Don't you get it? I was fine! I was getting along! Things were okay and then you swoop in again, tell me that everything I'd believed about my life was a lie. That you owned the building in which I lived, owned the company where I worked, employed the people I thought were my friends...!" She buried her face in her hands. "Oh, what's the use! You don't get it!"

He pulled her closer, ignoring her when she fought back. "And you think your life is out of control and that's making you more vulnerable."

Callie sagged against him when she heard that he truly understood. "You don't play fair, Zahir," she sobbed.

He rested his chin on top of her head. "No. I play to win. And I'm going to win you Callie."

They sat like that for a long time. Not speaking. Just thinking.

It was in that moment that he knew what he had to do.

Chapter 13

The following day was a much more mysterious excursion. This time, they had to fly across the country though. And that just made Callie more anxious.

"Where are we?" Callie asked as Zahir walked with her from the limousine. He had Luca in one arm and Callie was holding onto his other. He slipped his hands down and captured hers as he said, "This is the Fortress of the Guards, an ancient fortress that was built partly by my ancestors in order to protect the land and the people. No one is allowed admittance to this fortress without permission from either myself or three other people." The guards in front of them saluted smartly as they held the doors open for their ruler.

"I've never heard of this place," Callie said, her eyes wide as she looked around at the old walls that looked like they'd taken a beating but were still standing strong. This was nothing like the palace she thought. Where Zahir's palace had elaborate tile work and marble columns, flooring made up of numerous kinds of materials, this fortress was made of stone. It wasn't meant to show off a ruler's wealth, it was meant to protect and defend.

"It isn't a secret, but we don't advertise that we have started using it again." They headed through long, dimly lit hallways that felt vaguely ominous. Thankfully, there were lights that lit the way and broke through the thickly oppressive darkness. The fortress might look old and antiquated but the modern conveniences had obviously been installed at some point. There was lighting and air-conditioning even though the air still felt slightly damp. Even that was an interesting perception since they were still in the desert. "Is there water nearby?" Callie asked

Zahir nodded his head. "There are underground wells and various access points throughout the fortress. It was one of the reasons why it was built here. The architects of this fortress wanted to ensure that the people the building protected would have access to water, which was one of the main ways that people died centuries ago. Lack of clean water could win a war more effectively than arrows or bullets."

Callie couldn't stop the shudder that ripped through her. It still continued to shock her the ways that people tortured others in order to gain power. "So why are we here?"

Luca's eyes were wide as he looked around, his chubby arm holding onto the back of his father's neck as he took in his new surroundings. "I like it!" Luca announced.

Zahir smiled, proud of his son. "The people you are about to meet are going to surprise you." He looked into Callie's eyes, trying to get her to grasp the significance of who they were about to meet. "I understand your fears about the war starting up and your anxiety over being vulnerable. The people you are about to meet, the people that you will be spending the next twenty-four hours with, are going to prove to you that there is an absolute dedication among the four, previously warring countries to maintain the current peace."

Callie opened her mouth to say something, but she wasn't exactly sure what to say.

At that moment, there was noise that seemed to be coming from the end of the hallway where they were standing. Suddenly, the doors at the end of this hallway opened up and bright sunshine flooded in, almost blinding the three of them.

"I guess they are already here," Zahir said. He chuckled slightly as he shook his head and moved further down the passageway.

Callie's eyes squinted as the intense, desert sunshine warmed everything up relatively quickly. The difference between the dim hallway and this large, open courtyard almost hurt her eyes. She slipped the sunglasses down from the top of her head to shield her eyes from the harsh glare. As soon as her eyes adjusted, she was startled to see three equally large men walking towards her. The stern expressions on each of their faces caused her to involuntarily move closer to Zahir. "Who are they?" she whispered to Zahir.

Zahir looked down at his wife, surprised that she didn't recognize the men. Then again, perhaps it wasn't such a surprise. Callie had endured a horrible ordeal five years ago. She probably tried very hard to block any sort of memory about that from her life. It was a coping mechanism that many people used, and he should have been aware of that.

"Callie, I would like to introduce you to Sheik Tarek bin Faisal of Tularia, Sheik Garon al Sharhi of Lurasa and Sheik Dassar bin Sarook of Altair." He paused as each man greeted her, lifting her delicate hand to his lips in a gentlemanly fashion.

Tarek smiled down at the lovely little lady. "It is indeed a pleasure to meet you. I understand that it was because of you that this ugly old buffoon decided to end this ridiculous war." He bowed over her hand once again. "I am completely in your debt.

If there is ever anything that you need, please do not hesitate to contact me. My people are truly thankful to you for putting up with this man for so long."

Dassar laughed at the exchange as he too took Callie's hand in greeting. "I believe that we are all in your debt. I don't know how you put up with him, but please continue to make him happy so that we can avoid any other altercations."

Garon agreed "Your patience in dealing with this ugly and annoying man must far exceed your incredible beauty."

Callie kept glancing up at Zahir's expression, noticing that he rolled his eyes at several of their comments. Luca wasn't as subtle. His little hands were covering his mouth as he tried to smother the giggles while each man greeted his mother.

"I don't think that I understand," she said, looking at each man and then back at Zahir.

Zahir took her hand and placed it right back on his arm, exactly where he preferred it to be. "I wanted you back. I knew that you wouldn't come back if there was a war going on so I figured out a way to stop the war."

Tarek nodded his head. "If it weren't for his ideas, and his initiation, we would all still be at war. More people would be losing their lives daily. But it was your husband who brought us all here to this place, showed us how we could stop this war."

Callie was stunned. She really wasn't sure exactly what to say. All four of these men were so powerful in their own countries, and they were crediting her with a cessation of the war? Here she was standing beside some of the most powerful men in the world, and they were thanking her? It all felt more than a little surreal.

Tarek changed the subject. "I hear that this little guy is a really good soccer player. I think we should see for ourselves."

Dassar and Garon both nodded their heads in agreement. "I saw the video. I'm on his team," he said, pointing to Luca.

Zahir turned to his son, looking at him with pride in his eyes. "Do you think we can take them on?"

Luca was grinning from ear to ear, his whole body wiggling with the excitement of playing soccer with these four enormous man. Not to mention, he wanted to show his father how good he was on the soccer field.

Callie watched with fascination as four men and one little boy converted what she suspected was a former military training field into an improvised soccer field. Furthermore, she could not believe how silly the normally stern and terrifying-looking men could be while trying to entertain her tiny son. Not to mention, the cheating between these men was hilarious.

One would kick the ball down the field and, because the four of them were so tall, one would pick Luca up and carry him down the field. All of them would kick and battle as the one carrying her son got him into position to kick the ball.

Sometimes they set Luca back down on the ground and let him chase the ball and kick it. In those cases the men would all cheer, laugh, and actually punch each other, as if those punches were congratulatory. Other times, whichever enormous man holding her son would swing her child through the air. Luca knew to keep his feet steady and the momentum of the swing would shoot the ball across the field.

A servant magically appeared and provided a chair as well as a glass filled with ice and the most delicious drink she'd ever had. So Callie was allowed to sit and watch the five males play a rambunctious if not exactly rule-abiding game of soccer. She laughed and cheered and, by the end of the game, had absolutely no idea who had won or even who was on either team. They all seem to change teams as the need arose in order to score a point. It was one of the most ridiculous soccer games she'd ever seen in her life, and also the funniest.

Luca hurried over to where she was sitting. As he approached, Callie knew exactly what was going to happen. Too many times, her little boy had been out on the field, racing back and forth, kicking the ball, cheering with his friends. He might be little, but he was also a very sweaty little boy. Sure enough, he threw himself into her arms, exhilarated by his success.

No matter how many times she cringed as his sweaty little body threw himself into her arms, she still loved his enthusiasm.

What she hadn't been anticipating was Zahir pulling her into his arms, plastering her linen clad body against his very sweaty one and kissing her until she was clinging to him. After a moment, she didn't mind. All she cared about was that the kiss continued.

The chuckles behind Zahir were her first indication that she had to stop kissing him. Peering around his body, she noticed that Dassar, Tarek and Garon were all staring at the two of them as they kissed. Tarek had even lifted Luca onto his shoulders. And the little traitor was rolling his eyes as his parents kissed.

He bent over Tarek's head as he explained, "They do this a lot."

Zahir turned around, his arms still around Callie's waist. "Don't you guys have something else you need to do?"

Garon, Tarek and Dassar all quickly shook their heads. "You are the master. We are all trying to learn from your technique," Tarek teased.

Dassar nudged Garon in the ribs. "If only we'd found Callie first, Zahir would never have stood a chance."

Garon chuckled and nodded his head. "It's too bad that she had to settle for second best."

Callie was so shocked at their words that she wasn't exactly sure what to say. So she was relieved when Zahir squeezed her waist, indicating that they were only teasing her. "Go find your own women!"

He then reached up and took Luca off of Tarek's shoulders. "And get your own kid too." Zahir ruffled Luca's hair. "This one is taken."

The three other men laughed. "So dinner tonight?"

Zahir nodded, holding Luca in his arms. "It should be ready within the hour."

Everyone agreed and they slowly dispersed, shoving each other as they bragged about how they'd scored a better point with Luca than the other man had before they separated. Callie glanced over her shoulder as Zahir pulled her towards one corner of the fortress. Each of the men were heading towards opposite corners of the courtyard in which they played soccer. "Why are they all going in different directions?"

Zahir took her hand as he carried Luca towards the section of the palace that sat on his land. "This fortress is built on the spot where the four countries intersect. It was built before our countries were formed, but as the centuries went by, the leaders of each country built their own section of the fortress. It was always intended to be used as a private place where the four leaders could get together and negotiate issues between the four countries. It's just been in the past 10 years when those negotiations had broken down. This fortress hadn't been used since the beginning of the war. But it has been the place where we've secretly met, away from the eyes of the world and the press, to figure out how we could end this war. So they each live in their country's section of the fortress while we're negotiating."

She nodded her head as she followed Zahir down the hallway. She was painfully self-conscious of the way he was still holding her hand as they walked, but each time she tried to pull her hand away, to put more space between them, he only held her hand more firmly.

And since Callie wasn't exactly sure what was going on, what she was going to do, or what was expected of her, she finally stopped trying to pull away. She was in a foreign country, not sure where she was, and she wanted to accept the security that his touch offered to her.

Dinner that evening was just as raucous as the soccer game had been. Gone were the severe, stern expressions that each man showed to the rest of the world. At this table, the teasing and jibes flipped across the table with abandon. It was obvious to Callie that these men more than respected each other. They were friends. And as the evening wore on, she understood that they were close friends. It underscored what Zahir was telling her previously about how the peace was more than just a treaty that had been signed by four countries. It felt like these men were dedicated to maintaining their friendship, and maintaining the peace.

That night, after Luca had gone to bed, she waited in the bedroom for Zahir. Her hands were twisting together nervously and she wasn't sure what to say or do. She was so used to pulling away from Zahir, from what he meant to her, that facing those emotions was leaving her more vulnerable than she'd like to be.

So when he stepped through the doors, she was startled and jerked in his direction.

"What's wrong, love?" he asked, moving over to her and taking her hands so she wasn't rubbing the skin raw any longer.

"You did it all for me, didn't you?" she asked softly, feeling like a fool. "And for Luca."

He knew exactly what she was asking. "Yes. I couldn't stand it any longer. I would have done it five years ago but the leadership wasn't right. I knew I couldn't get the previous rulers to go along with my plan." He kissed her fingertips. "When they passed away, I pulled the four of us together and showed them a plan, a way to get this war behind us."

She was so tired of crying but this time, she was ready. She couldn't believe all she'd learned today and how light-hearted she felt at the moment. It was as if the weight of a heavy problem was gone. And she knew that was exactly what she had to say.

"Thank you," she whispered, looking down at her hands that were twisting together. "Thank you for ending the war and…" she stumbled on this part. "Thank you for…"

She looked out the window, not sure how to say this. It still scared her but he deserved to know the truth. "And thank you for not giving up on us."

She felt his hands slide onto her silk covered shoulders. She wasn't wearing one of his large shirts tonight. She was in one of the beautiful nightgowns and a silk robe that had been packed for her.

"Did the others reassure you about the future?" he asked gently, his deep voice sliding over her softly.

"Yes." She nodded her head, still looking out into the dark night. "Yes, they reassured me but…"

"Stop Callie," he told her and turned her around. "No. I can't guarantee the future. No, I can't guarantee that nothing else will happen to you or Luca or myself or any of the other children we will have in the future." He ignored her weepy laughter at his arrogant assumption. "I can only show you what I've done to make you and the rest of the country safe. There are horrible people in this world. But I can eliminate some of the risks. Not all," he cautioned.

She nodded. "I understand."

He lifted her head so that she was looking at him. "Do you?"

"Yes," she sobbed and leaned against him. For the first time, she was initiating an embrace. "Yes. I understand and I'm sorry that I doubted you."

He wrapped his arms around her, closing his eyes as the implication of her words hit him. "And?" he coaxed when it seemed that she wouldn't continue.

Callie smiled against his hard chest. The man really was arrogant, she thought. He wouldn't settle for anything less than full disclosure. Which was probably what made him such an amazing ruler, but it would make him an annoying husband. "And," she started off, "I think that has been enough revelations for one night."

She pulled out of his arms and sauntered away, ignoring the growl from Zahir almost directly behind her. She was prepared to run, to get out of his reach but once again, she hesitated. Always her downfall, she thought as she yelped when his arms tossed her up into the air, her legs swinging out while he spun her around, getting a better grip on her. She laughed at his growl as he carried her over to the enormous bed. "Callie, if you don't tell me the words I want to hear, I'm going to have to tickle them out of you," he told her firmly.

She wrapped her arms around his neck, enjoying this playful side of him. She'd seen it when they were together the first time but things had been too tense, too serious over the past two weeks. This side of him had been hidden.

"I'm not saying anything else. You're too spoiled already. I have to be the balancing influence on both you and Luca."

She screamed and tried to wiggle away from him when his teeth nipped at her neck while his hands tickled her. "Tell me, woman," he commanded, holding her right where he wanted her.

Callie shook her head, her stomach aching from her laughter. "No. I have nothing else to say to you."

He lifted his head and looked down into her beautiful, laughing features. "Is that really how you want to play this?" he asked and Callie's stomach muscles tensed even more as she saw the promise in his dark eyes.

"Yes," she whispered, her body already preparing for whatever he might dish out to her.

Zahir smiled, his eyes moving down her silk covered figure with wicked intent. "I was hoping you'd say that."

Callie gasped and sighed and a long time later, when she was naked and completely sated as she snuggled into his arms, she whispered, "I love you."

Zahir rolled over her once again, his body already preparing for yet another bout of making this woman scream out with pleasure. "I love you too, Callie. And I promise, I won't let anything happen to you. You're my wife and I love you more than I can say."

Callie thought about the three other men that were sleeping somewhere in the fortress and all that had been revealed today. "You ended a war for me," she whispered. "There was a woman in history who started a war but," she lifted her hands, letting her fingers slide through his black hair slowly, "I think that ending the war to get me back is so much more romantic." And she showed him how much she loved him one more time.

Excerpt from The Sheik's Angry Bride, Book 4 in The War, Love, and Harmony Series

Layla smoothed the long, black gloves up over her arms and elbows, ignoring the pains in her stomach. She would not give in to the nausea. This is what she had been trained for. This moment, this role…all her life she'd been told that this was her purpose. Everything she'd trained for her whole life was for this moment. All details of the contract negotiated, each aspect of the agreement argued about and finalized, every line of the contract ultimately signed by the appropriate people. Not by her, of course! No, she hadn't been called into any office to sign the agreement. But that didn't matter. This moment represented everything she'd been trained for since birth.

She took a deep breath and focused all of her attention on ensuring that there were no wrinkles in her dress or her gloves, that the diamond bracelet on her wrist didn't show the clasp and refused to contemplate what was about to happen. Her gloved hand reached up and smoothed her hair, then stopped. There was so much hairspray on her right now, the friction of touching it in any way might light her head on fire.

Layla might have smiled at the idea if she weren't so terrified inside. That didn't stop the image from forming though. She could just picture her fiancé's face when he walked into this meeting room only to discover a ball of flames instead of his fiancée. Of course, Layla would stand perfectly upright, a smile of greeting on her overly made up features as she bowed and tried not to let the flames from her hair touch any of the medals on her intended's immaculate and exalted chest. But that was what she'd been trained all of her life for – to look acceptable at every moment of the day and produce heirs. No other reason – just to adorn her husband's arm and act as a walking womb.

A burst of hysterical laughter threatened but she took a deep breath, trying hard to remain composed despite her mind's overly active imagination at work right at the moment.

It wouldn't do for her to be caught laughing when she met her future husband for the first timeF she thought and then cringed inwardly because even her inner dialogue now sounded like her mother, admonishing her for being silly. Regardless, she pulled her shoulders back and took a deep breath, trying to snap out of this terror she was feeling. No, it definitely wouldn't do to appear to be smiling. And laughing? Out of the question, she told herself mentally. A pleasant expression was all that was needed during this meeting. Anything more might offend, anything less my insult.

Over and over, this had been drilled into her throughout her life to the point where she now could breathe in, breathe out, and then look up with the perfectly serene expression on her face that she'd been forced to practice while growing up.

She was also painfully aware that smiling too brightly might cause her makeup to crack. Goodness, wouldn't that be silly? She could see the headlines tomorrow morning… "A chunk of the princess' face fell to the floor after she laughed!"

No, she mentally shook herself. That wouldn't do, either. Serenity, she chanted to herself. She'd practiced this look in the mirror so often, it should come naturally to her by now. Breathe in. Breathe out. Lift the chin. Hands calm. Spine straight. And don't throw up on the man! For goodness sake, don't throw up!

The doors at the other end of the hallway opened up and she pulled her shoulders back. Showtime, she thought, and suppressed the resentment that was welling up inside of her.

She waited patiently, her light blue eyes glancing across each man's face as he stepped through the doors, wondering if that was her future husband. She was relieved to be wearing the high necked, black satin sheath dress so that her pounding heart wouldn't be noticed. This was the night her hopes and dreams were to die. This was the night when all of her silly girl fantasies were obliterated.

This was the night when she met her new owner.

Garon stepped through the double doors just as his guards separated to the right and left. His eyes moved through the crowd of people standing inside the room, taking it all in. But his gaze skidded to a screeching halt as he took in the trembling beauty standing in the middle of the room. There was no way he could miss the fact that this was his bride. The other guests, including her mother and father, were all standing near the walls while this stunning beauty stood in the center watching him with her lovely fairy eyes and soft, full lips, a slender figure clad all in black from her neck right down to her dainty toes and her long fingers.

Two things occurred to him at that moment. The first was that his exquisite fiancée had come to their first meeting dressed for a funeral which amused him. He had no doubt that the message was intended.

But the other issue was this woman's beauty, which was quite startling. He'd seen formal pictures of her, of course. The negotiations for this marriage had taken place over the past several months so he had known what Layla Alfarsi looked like. But he was startled by the impact of her, which was not something he had anticipated. He wanted to be attracted to his wife, that was a given. What he hadn't foreseen were the other reactions that hit him like a punch in the gut.

This feeling, this instinctual predatory anticipation that surged up inside of him as he approached his future bride was not anticipated. And he wasn't sure it was welcome either.

The entire reason for this meeting was to get to know his bride before the wedding. Not to toss her over his shoulder so he could carry her away to a private place and have his way with her.

Reining in his near blinding need to possess this woman, he stopped directly in front of her. Looking down at her, he was surprised at how small she felt. According to the dossier he'd been given on Layla Alfarsi, she was supposed to be five feet, five inches tall. But this woman, even in heels, barely came to his shoulder. Her slight form, her willowy figure, probably made her appear smaller, he thought.

"Good evening, Layla," he started off. He reached down and took her hand, irritated with the long gloves. He wanted to rip them off of her, to feel her soft skin and explore those pink lips. But she might get offended by that, he supposed.

All in due time, he reminded himself. Very soon, this woman would be his. And he could explore all of that trembling courage at his leisure.

"Good evening, Your Highness," she replied, dipping into a curtsy and bowing her head.

Layla couldn't believe how hard it was to rise from that simple gesture but her legs were trembling and her heart pounding so hard, she was actually worried that she might fall onto the floor at this man's feet. He must have sensed her trepidation because his hand tightened on her fingers, helping her to rise out of the curtsy. When she was once more standing in front of him, she knew that the polite thing to do was to thank him silently but she simply couldn't look up at him. Not this man!

He was too…everything! Shock waves rocketed throughout her body as the heat from his hand seemed to be melting the silk of her black gloves where he continued to touch her. She'd tried to pull her hand away, but he wouldn't release her fingers.

Layla felt trapped by this man. He was barely touching her but there was something about him, a sense deep inside of her that told her she should run as fast and as hard as she could away from him.

But her training kicked in once more and she straightened her shoulders. Waiting.

And waiting. In fact, everyone in the room seemed to be silent, waiting.

"We will stand here all night, my beauty, until you look at me," he told her in a voice that only she could hear.

Layla's heart, already pounding fast, went into triple time with his words. Look at him? She wanted to run away! She wanted to hide behind the enormous plant in the corner. She wanted to whip her hand out from his grasp and step backwards so there was more space between the two of them. She absolutely did not want to look up at him.

But this was her duty. He'd commanded, she must obey. Gritting her teeth, she forced her eyes higher. And higher! Goodness, he was tall!

When her blue eyes finally met his, that horrible trembling increased even more. His black gaze looked down at her and that need to flee, to hide, intensified. But something else also rose up. Something that saved her from making a fool of herself and bringing dishonor upon her family.

Anger!

Oh, the wonderful, heat-encouraging, bubbling anger was her saving grace. Gritting her teeth, she stared right back at this man, daring him to…to do whatever it was he might do! She had no idea of his intentions, nor was she going to ask. She simply waited for him, challenging him with her blue eyes as they fought a battle of wills.

Garon's stomach muscles clenched and his body reacted to that angry gaze. Until a few months ago, he'd never really contemplated his wife and the traits he might want in that woman. Nor had there been any discussion during the negotiations about Layla's preferences, her temperament. He was simply assured that she had been raised to know her duty, her responsibilities. Testing had been done to ensure her fertility and that was the end of that conversation. All the negotiations from that point on were monetary and political. The exchange of this woman from her family to his would be a boon to both sides of the negotiating table.

Every feral and predatory cell in his body reacted to her challenge, to those striking, blue eyes glaring up at him. He wanted to both subdue her rebellion while at the same time, set her passion free. The unexpected pleasure he found in just looking at her shot through him and he had to stop himself from ordering everyone out of the room but this one woman.

List of Elizabeth Lennox Books

The Texas Tycoon's Temptation

The Royal Cordova Trilogy
Escaping a Royal Wedding
The Man's Outrageous Demands
Mistress to the Prince

The Attracelli Family Series
Never Dare a Tycoon
Falling For the Boss
Risky Negotiations
Proposal to Love
Love's Not Terrifying
Romantic Acquisition

The Billionaire's Terms: Prison or Passion
The Sheik's Love Child
The Sheik's Unfinished Business
The Greek Tycoon's Lover
The Sheik's Sensuous Trap
The Greek's Baby Bargain
The Italian's Bedroom Deal
The Billionaire's Gamble
The Tycoon's Seduction Plan
The Sheik's Rebellious Mistress
The Sheik's Missing Bride
Blackmailed by the Billionaire
The Billionaire's Runaway Bride
The Billionaire's Elusive Lover
The Intimate, Intricate Rescue

The Sisterhood Trilogy
The Sheik's Virgin Lover
The Billionaire's Impulsive Lover
The Russian's Tender Lover
The Billionaire's Gentle Rescue

The Tycoon's Toddler Surprise
The Tycoon's Tender Triumph

The Friends Forever Series
The Sheik's Mysterious Mistress
The Duke's Willful Wife
The Tycoon's Marriage Exchange

The Sheik's Secret Twins
The Russian's Furious Fiancée
The Tycoon's Misunderstood Bride

Love By Accident Series
The Sheik's Pregnant Lover
The Sheik's Furious Bride
The Duke's Runaway Princess

The Russian's Pregnant Mistress

The Lovers Exchange Series
The Earl's Outrageous Lover
The Tycoon's Resistant Lover

The Sheik's Reluctant Lover
The Spanish Tycoon's Temptress

The Berutelli Escape
Resisting The Tycoon's Seduction
The Billionaire's Secretive Enchantress

The Big Apple Brotherhood
The Billionaire's Pregnant Lover
The Sheik's Rediscovered Lover

The Tycoon's Defiant Southern Belle

The Sheik's Dangerous Lover (Novella)

The Thorpe Brothers
His Captive Lover
His Unexpected Lover
His Secretive Lover
His Challenging Lover

The Sheik's Defiant Fiancée (Novella)
The Prince's Resistant Lover (Novella)
The Tycoon's Make-Believe Fiancée (Novella)

The Friendship Series
The Billionaire's Masquerade
The Russian's Dangerous Game
The Sheik's Beautiful Intruder

The Love and Danger Series – Romantic Mysteries
Intimate Desires
Intimate Caresses
Intimate Secrets
Intimate Whispers

The Alfieri Saga
The Italian's Passionate Return (Novella)
Her Gentle Capture
His Reluctant Lover
Her Unexpected Admirer
Her Tender Tyrant
Releasing the Billionaire's Passion (Novella)
His Expectant Lover

The Sheik's Intimate Proposition (Novella)

The Hart Sisters Trilogy
The Billionaire's Secret Marriage
The Italian's Twin Surprise (USA Today™ Best Seller!)
The Forbidden Russian Lover (USA Today™ Best Seller!)

The War, Love, and Harmony Series
Fighting with the Infuriating Prince (Novella)
Dancing with the Dangerous Prince (Novella)
The Sheik's Secret Bride
The Sheik's Angry Bride
The Sheik's Blackmailed Bride
The Sheik's Convenient Bride

The Boarding School Series – September 2015 to January 2016
The Boarding School Series Introduction
The Greek's Forgotten Wife
The Duke's Blackmailed Bride
The Russian's Runaway Bride
The Sheik's Baby Surprise
The Tycoon's Captured Heart